FORGOTTEN ONES

DRABBLES OF MYTH AND LEGEND

AN EERIE RIVER PUBLISHING ANTHOLOGY

FORGOTTEN ONES

Paperback ISBN: 978-1-7770410-2-1
Hardcover ISBN: 978-1-7770410-0-7
Digital ISBN: 978-1-7770410-3-8

Edited by Alanna Robertson-Webb
Cover design by Michelle River
Book Formatting by Michelle River
Title page art by Aina Tolero

When you are finished reading this collection of stories please take a moment and review it on Amazon, Goodreads, and/or BookBub.

AVAILABLE NOW FROM

EERIE RIVER PUBLISHING

STORMING AREA 51: HORROR AT THE GATE

DON'T LOOK: 12 STORIES OF BITE SIZED HORROR

COMING SOON: 2020

IT CALLS FROM THE FOREST

IT CALLS FROM THE FOREST: VOLUME II

IT CALLS FROM THE SKY

IT CALLS FROM THE SEA

That is the gods' work, spinning threads of death
through the lives of mortal men,
and all to make a song for those to come.

HOMER, *The Odyssey*

Table of Contents

Dedicated to all our families and friends. Those that have stood beside us, and often behind us while we type away, bringing us coffee and listening to us talk about our characters as if they were real; because they are.

Thank you for believing in us.

FOREWORD

We want to take a moment and thank you for purchasing this book, for supporting Eerie River Publishing and for experiencing the talented authors we've featured.

The collection you are about to dive into is comprised of over two hundred drabbles, which were created by over ninety authors from around the globe.

These seemingly simple, exactly one hundred word stories will transport you to a time beyond memory, a place where old gods ruled and creatures of myth walked among us. They will darken your soul and titillate your senses.

Be warned, for the stories within these pages are not for the faint of heart or the easily triggered. Some will find them horrifying in nature, while others will find them comforting. For these are drabbles of a different kind.

May you be forever entertained,
Eerie River Publishing

THE CONJURING
S. C. MORGAN

Zebeth traced the markings, all jagged lines and symbols, in a circle on the floor. Smoke wafted up in a haze, swirling in a vortex over the markings.

Feeling its presence she watched the orb of light pulse as it grew larger. Streaks of energy swirled through the air, giving way to a dark, boiling cloud.

A misshapen face emerged, staring back at her.

"What would you wish of me, sorceress?"

Drawing a dagger from its sheath Zebeth stared at the djinn. She exhaled as she pulled the blade across her hand, drawing blood.

"I would have revenge."

www.facebook.com/SCMorganAuthor/
Twitter: @ScmorganAuthor

WHAT BLASPHEMY?
BRYAN DYKE

The wraps go on tight over my throat, the stench of natron and myrrh invading my nose. The hyena-faced priest looks down at me and smiles.

Behind him, the god stands. Chaos crawling. He is a robe of inky shadow, adorned with a smiling golden mask. Not unlike Anubis, but far more wicked. Older. This is not real. More wraps bind me tight. Now the final passes, the thick bandages cover my mouth and eyes.

Not real.

My sweat freezes, but my heart pounds like the deep drums of Stygia.

"Seal the tomb," the metallic voice orders.

AZATHOTH
K.T. TATE

It was flutes that woke us, high and lilting in the frigid silence. The shadow, dark and not quite human, passed over each tent, drawing us out. Dazed, we stumbled onto the icy plateau. Eldritch light bathed us, pouring from a fracture in the heavens. The sky, cobwebbed cracks crossing over our world, revealing its form.

Some of us screamed, others clawed at their eyes, but in the end we all danced to the maddening flutes. That atrocity from beyond reality looked down on us with idiot eyes, unfocused. The tundra stained with blood, just the first of many sacrifices.

https://eldritch-hollow.com/

THE MOON WILL RISE
ROBIN BRAID

Lashed to the towering witch stone the girl's red hair hung black in the moonlight, shadowing her eyes from the faceless forms that circled. The wind fell away, the woods grew silent, and before her a hooded figure mumbled incantations in a tongue seldom heard across the centuries.

A hand was raised, a bright blade flashing swiftly as it cut deep. The girl made no sound. Her head dropped, and the earth beneath her feet grew darker still. Through twisted branches the moon flared brightly, illuminating a ragged shape at the edge of the clearing.

"Behold children, she has risen."

www.twitter.com/robinbraid

Sleep Tight

Sarah Matthews

"I can't go to sleep, I'm scared," said the boy.

"I've already checked under your bed and in your closet. I promise you, there's no monsters," said his mother.

"But, Mommy…" cried the boy.

"No 'buts'! Now go to b…" The mother's words were cut short as an inky figure fell upon her from above, claws and teeth slashing. The mother let out a scream that ended in a gurgle. The boy dove under his blankets, holding his breath as thudding footsteps lurched towards his bed.

"You forgot to check the ceiling," snarled the Boogeyman, yanking back the covers.

Twitter @superbfinch

SEARCH FOR HISTORY
CHRIS BANNOR

The boy in his arms babbled and cried, but he didn't look behind them. All he could do was keep moving.

He had come searching for history, but had found something far worse. He used to believe that for every myth, every story, there was an origin that was not so fantastical. He had come to find those truths and share them with the world.

What he found was far worse than the legends, because the truth was grotesque and horrid. The stories, as they were printed, were real.

So he raced, clutching his son, failing to outrun the Erlking.

Facebook: @chrisbannorauthor
www.ChrisBannor.com

Chosen

Joshua E. Borgmann

For millennia her employers, arcane priests with their chanting, hidden covens, dusty grimoires, and blood sacrifices, had failed. Yet she, a nerd with a keyboard, had succeeded with only lines of code. Now her skin rippled from unnamable creeping frequencies emanating from infected electronic devices, her sanity caved from what she unleashed.

Tentacles reaching from screens, masses staring into distorted space, her employers' eyes dribbling down their cheeks. In the swirling chaos on the horizon mountainous forms appeared, feeding her images of abomination. Cities would become twisted, inside out, and upside down.

They kept whispering, "This is for you, Mother."

HACKLES

MARK ANTHONY SMITH

I can scarcely read the scrawl as a bony claw falls heavily on my shoulder. The unknown breath stinks of rotting fish, its grip tightens as I stumble with the invocation. The words are ancient, and the dark is getting darker. My mouth is dry.

I feel terror rising in my chest.

If I don't read then the ancient, scaly thing will impale me on its talons. If I carry on I'll give rise to other monstrosities, perhaps even more persuasive and terrible.

I pause, that hairy muzzle pressing into the back of my neck. I feel my hackles rise.

Twitter: @MarkAnthonySm16
Facebook: Mark Anthony Smith- Author

SLEEK NELLIE
SARAH MATTHEWS

Roman wasn't afraid as he entered Sleek Nellie's Grotto.

Not when the door he'd entered through vanished behind him, and not when he heard the splash of Sleek Nellie sliding into the water and swimming towards him.

When she leapt from the water and stood before him Roman wasn't afraid. Not of her scaly skin and dripping green hair, not of her clawed hands, not of her rows of serrated teeth.

What about when Sleek Nellie swiped at him, ripping the skin from his body? When she bit into him like a freshly peeled, juicy apple?

Then Roman was afraid.

Twitter @superbfinch

NIDSTANG

Tor-Anders Ulven

At first I just laughed. I mean, it was so extremely bizarre. A stuffed horse's head erected on a pole. But then I noticed the blood in the snow. As I moved closer the stench of death filled my nostrils. The poor creatures' skin was pulled down, revealing rotting flesh underneath.

"Nidstang!" my neighbor Harald yelled. "A curse upon you and your house!"

It was just a neighbor's quarrel, a little dispute over a tree. Now I can hardly move. My skin's covered in black, oozing wounds. My wife stopped moving hours ago, the foul liquid filling her lungs.

Nidstang.

https://www.facebook.com/hyperobscure/
https://www.reddit.com/user/hyperobscura

THE NAHANNI

L.P. HERNANDEZ

In the far north the sun shines, always or never. Giants once roamed this valley, the Natives say, and left behind a trail of headless warriors. They abandoned the fresh water, the plentiful game, taking only their legends and a fear of tall trees. For generations they hovered on the outskirts of the valley, longing for the riches within.

Slowly the Natives return to their ancestral land, finding no evidence of giants.

The Nahanni is peaceful, on the surface.

Beneath, in the blackest soil, a long hibernation ends, and a furious appetite is stirring.

The valley will tremble once more.

www.lphernandez.com

HUNGER

REGINA KENNEY

I rose from below to grasp human ankles and drag them down. Hungry for flesh, I performed spins, breaking water in sprays, turning until blood stained the water.

How I loved the stories of my great scales, my lovely teeth, and the strength of my clutch. My terrible name was whispered between passing strangers.

Then men talked too much and visitors ceased. Forced to suck on slugs for decades, I grew weak.

Today a splash came. Towards the light, I saw two wriggling legs.

How many years have gone by? Enough to forget. Enough to swim in my waters again.

Twitter: @Regina_Kenney
Instagram: @Regina_Kenney

Book Wyrm
Kimberly Rei

The library was creepy at night. Jen called it peaceful, but Elijah hated the evening shift, especially in the winter when it got so dark so fast.

He was making his final round, putting off the Reserved Room. He had told Jen there was whispering in there. She laughed at him, as always.

Fear jammed his throat as he turned the latch. Head, then shoulders, slipped past the door.

Jen wasn't there to hear his strangled scream as long claws yanked Elijah off his feet. She didn't hear the crunch of a different sort of librarian enjoying a snack break.

http://tales.studiorei.org/

Lucy's Friend
Joel R. Hunt

"Imaginary friends are perfectly normal at Lucy's age."

"Even if they're not human?"

"You mean it's an animal?"

Mr. and Mrs. Harris looked to one another. They unfolded one of Lucy's drawings, full of angry, black scrawls and jagged teeth.

"She calls it Ialdagorth the Devourer. She talks about it in her sleep, saying that it's approaching, gaining power. Her drawings are, well, getting bigger."

"Bigger than this?"

Mr. Harris gestured to the window. Peering outside, Dr. Parker saw Lucy hard at work with her crayons. She had engulfed the entire street in a black, hungry maw, open and waiting.

https://twitter.com/JoelRHunt1
https://www.reddit.com/r/JRHEvilInc/

Broken Board
Michelle River

The planchette burned like hot coals against my fingertips. Unable to move I watched, frozen in fear, as soul-tearing screams were wretched from Alanna's lungs. Her bones snapped, ligaments popping painfully. Her body contorted in front of me, the old ouija board cracking.

A shadow oozed from the broken board, the ink pooling away from the letters and seeping towards her like smoke from a smudging stick. Panic consumed me as she made a final gasp, her body falling limply to the floor.

The shadow turned to me.

"Thank you."

Thick tendrils of smoke grasped me, the shadow consuming me.

www.facebook.com/michelleriverauthor/
www.twitter.com/MRiver_Writes

ALLFATHER

ELIN OLAUSSON

They took her to the Rock on the thirty-third day of the Hunger, once people had started dying. Her bare feet were dragged through the snow. Around her the men chanted, low humming voices calling His name.

At the Rock they lifted the furs from her, pushing her onto her back. Their faces were gaunt and wild, their mouths moving as one. The chanting grew louder, and a new voice joined them.

An ancient voice, deep as the sea, whispering Galdr. His shadow towered over them all, his one eye on her as the knife was lifted.

Odin, Odin, Odin.

www.elinolausson.com
Twitter: @elin_writes

THE CARCOSA MASQUERADE
SARAH MATTHEWS

The costumed courtiers bowed before The King in Yellow.

"Unmask," he commanded.

"Your Majesty, I wear no mask," said a courtier. The crowd gasped.

The King descended from his throne, the tatters of his saffron robes flapping in the night breeze.

"We all wear masks," he said.

He stretched out razor sharp talons, digging into the courtier's face, severing skin from muscle. The courtier let out a laugh like a scream, or a scream like a laugh, it was impossible to tell.

"Now the rest of you: unmask!" roared The King.

The court rang with the sound of rending flesh.

Twitter @superbfinch.

LIFE CHANGES
N.M. BROWN

Our Timothy is in a bit of an awkward phase. He's shorter than others his age, and suffers from deformations. Yet he's extraordinarily intelligent, an old soul.

A boy rang our doorbell on Timothy's thirteenth birthday, one who looked identical to my son but without defects.

"Mother, it's me!" He squeaked.

Timothy charged upon seeing him, plunging my fabric scissors into the boy's neck.

As the sweat runs down my back from digging this grave, even as I recall how his eyes changed to black just before the attack, I must remember that I'm his Mother.

I love him.

PETRA
WENDY CHEAIRS

The children curled together, fattened over the months leading to the stars aligning and becoming prepared for the ritual. They knew nothing, innocent to the end. They followed the priestess willingly towards the stone area, the hard dirt circled up to the great portal. The world needed the pool refilled, allowing the goddess to remain protecting the people. Each child lined the outer circle waiting their turn, opening their arms to the knife's edge. Blood spilled into the empty pool, the pool of the goddess. Al-Uzza smiled upon her people, accepting the blood to fertilize the land and those within.

https://www.facebook.com/AuthorWendyCheairs/
https://indigowriter.com/

THE KELPIE
T.J. LEA

I watched as a fool stepped closer to the water's edge, responding to the calls of a beautiful woman in distress. She begged, cried, called his name as the watery trap enclosed around him. When he grabbed her slimy palms, his fate was sealed. Her smile twisting with her form, humanity fading as the mane sprung forth, watery tendrils gripping his skin so tight it ripped flesh from bone. As his eyes met the malformed face, white orbs and an inhuman grin the last thing he will witness, I feel elation that the Kelpie shall feed well on this night.

www.facebook.com/tjayleawriter
Twitter: @tjaylea

SACRIFICE
CALLUM PEARCE

His name was Sacrifice. Born and raised to bleed on the altar, destined to open a path to the underworld. As blood poured from his wrists, onto the painted symbols below, he could hear demons scraping through the earth. He heard them coming closer, making a route to this world for the mistress of darkness.

The demons didn't scare him, nor the Queen of Hell. It was the humans that terrified him the most. They created and raised him, they brought him here to this place. Now they stood over him, eager and hungry, slicing him to call to her.

Iä Iä Cthulhu fhtagn!
K.T. Tate

My discoveries have left me at the edge of sanity. We should've refused, but the museum was waiting. The ancient culture discovered was abhorrent, partaking in depraved rituals for their accursed god, their caves a maze of unimaginable artifacts.

Then the dreams came, reflecting what we'd learned. Men cavorting with squamous things, blasphemous songs calling their god up from the depths. Nightmares burned away by daylight, though their shadows remained.

But I've discovered a horrifying truth: That tentacled monstrosity is not their god.

He is their priest.

Which begs the question, to what does such an aberration bend its knee?

THE NUCKELAVEE
DREW STARLING

Two soldiers were sent to the isles of Orkney. Reports of massacred livestock and children gone missing sent panic through the land, and for three days and nights they searched for the one called Nuckelavee.

On a winter morning it appeared in the fog. A skinless man on a skinless horse, a single red eye to guide it. Its vine-thin arms dragged lifelessly on the ground. Its stench so foul that the grass wilted as it approached. The Nuckelavee cackled, and croaked out these words:

"Choose one man to die."

The men each chose each other, and the Nuckelavee obliged.

Twitter @ScaryStarling

THE MOUNTAIN
JACEK WILKOS

After many days of climbing he finally reached the top of the mountain. The wind whipped his face with hundreds of icy needles. The legends were true, he found a stone with runes carved in it. He took out a dagger, made an incision on his palm and put it on the rock. Flowing blood filled the carvings of the inscription, letter by letter. He closed his eyes, praying to the gods. It's the last hope for his people. As the last rune filled with crimson, the mountain began to tremble. It worked: the Great Old One was waking up.

https://www.facebook.com/Jacek.W.Wilkos/

αvατροπή

MATTHEW A CLARKE

As I sit, wondering where we went so wrong, a sudden, piercing siren assaults me.

It's a sound I have never heard before, a sound I hoped I'd never hear. I weep a solitary tear, the doors to the Pantheon swing inward.

"My King, they have breached our gates. Athena is slain."

"Very well," is all I can manage, as I pass Hermes.

I step outside where the cries of battle and the shriek of steel choke the air, pausing between the marble columns with lightning in my heart.

These men know not what they do.

They shall all burn.

www.facebook.com/fotc87

MARY HAD A LITTLE LAMB
JOEL R. HUNT

McCready marched towards the barn as fast as his aging legs could manage, shotgun under one arm, flashlight raised in the other. He had spotted someone – something – heading inside. They had appeared almost naked, tall and lithe and bathed in moonlight, a ram's skull covering their face.

McCready forced open the barn door, then reeled at the scene.

His animals had torn themselves apart. The floor was soaked in red. Stretched out between teeth and horns, glistening, their entrails formed the shape of a pentagram. Only his ewe, Mary, had been spared.

She lay safe in the centre, freshly pregnant.

https://twitter.com/JoelRHunt1
https://www.reddit.com/r/JRHEvilInc/

Robin Never Finished Her Bigfoot Video

Ann Wycoff

This isn't real!

The shaggy woman-gorilla was taller than a rearing grizzly, and heavier by far. Milk oozed from her pendulous breasts, aching to be drank from.

It's a suit!

The anthropoid seized her.

Robin soon believed.

Yellow eyes, broad fangs, worms and rotten nuts for breath.

Shadows clawed up from the campfire into the night. Robin screamed, kicking and lashing out with superhuman strength granted by fear.

The giant ignored her efforts, cradling her new baby with huge paws, freakish compared with her wiry arms.

Joy.

Mother cooed as she lumbered away with silent footfalls into the misty forest.

www.annwycoff.com

Omen Owl

Kerry E.B. Black

The Omen Owl screeches, but I'll not answer its call.

I've an ancestral gold dagger, an Aztec artifact. I'll plunge it into that feathered beast's chest and dig out its heart. I will feel it pump in my palm, once, twice, but before the third pulse I'll tear into it with my teeth. Its blood will congeal upon my chin; that way the fiendish fowl can't drag me to the Underworld.

The Omen Owl swoops.

I lunge.

Its feathers brush my cheek, its talons rake my chest. Its beak cracks my ribs and extracts my heart.

It beats once, twice...

https://www.goodreads.com/author/show/
7874880.Kerry_E_B_Black
https://twitter.com/BlackKerryblick

COME PLAY

GABRIELLA BALCOM

Nine-year-old Fumio heard splashing, and ran toward the Mogami River. Glimpsing children playing in the water he smiled, but his eyes widened when he neared them.

They had odd, yellowish-blue skin.

Although child-sized, the beings in front of him weren't human. They had monkey faces, wore turtle shells on their backs, and had liquid-filled depressions on the tops of their heads.

"Come play," they invited, beckoning eagerly to him.

Fumio hesitated, biting his lip, but their laughter and friendly smiles reassured him as he waded into the river.

The kappa surrounded him, for after cucumbers children were their favorite food.

https://m.facebook.com/GabriellaBalcom.lonestarauthor

MISFORTUNE OF THE NAGUAL
DEREK DUNN

The musky scent of copal resin wafted from the candle in Aapo's hand. He followed the flame, hoping to find food.

Yum Kaax, the forest's protector, should guide him, but it was only a myth. He'd been searching all day to no avail.

Suddenly, a deer appeared. Aapo raised his spear. The weapon pierced the animal's hide, dropping it to the ground. He pushed through the grass to find a woman, not a deer, lying lifeless before him.

Aapo fell to his knees. The tales were true, but instead of food he'd found a Nagual, a shapeshifter of the night.

Twitter: @DerekTDunn

You Sleep, I Cry

C. Marry Hulman

With a wet, gut-wrenching sound the head slowly tore from the body. Rising above the graves, entrails dragging from its neck.

Lintang crawled backward, startled at the sight of the Leyak. The single eye focused on her, the putrid stench of death wafting past. She was safe, but it had scared her all the same.

Pickaxe in hand she continued her work, the treasure foremost on her mind. The Leyak moved, but she ignored it.

Suddenly it screamed.

Mouth gaping it attacked her, sharp fangs digging into her belly.

She was supposed to be safe, Leyaks only attacked pregnant women.

https://wisconsinnoir.wixsite.com/wi

The Imp

Michael D. Nadeau

Sean was in trouble, and no one could help. Only he could feel the tiny claws digging into his skin, the acrid breath on his neck. Only he could see the shriveled creature on his shoulder, hear the whispered words it spoke to him.

He found it in the woods, caught in the undergrowth and pleading for help. Sean freed it, and it crawled up his back, perching on his shoulder. It promised it would help him in return.

Now Sean's boss, who had fired him, was on his knees begging.

Now slice his throat Sean! The imp whispered gleefully.

APHRODITE A.D.
BRYAN DYKE

The priests and priestesses of ivory temples sacrificed bulls to Aphrodite. They poured blood in the field and sowed the Earth with red splendor, her courtesans making love upon divans in mountainous palaces that overlooked lakes and warm vales.

Now the air smelled of burned tires and white phosphorous, the vales tainted by red fire and black ash.

Aphrodite held her beloved blade and wiped the ichor of void-things on her leg.

Shadows stirred.

You shall be a Goddess of War.

Her only regret was her foes did not bleed, and there would be no succor for the lost Earth.

THE GREEN CHILDREN
T.J. LEA

istory books say they came out of a pit in an ancient village, their skin green and their hunger for kidney beans beyond belief.

"An underground place always in twilight," they claimed, the ringing of a bell ushering them to this world.

The books usually end there. However, one account still remains concealed from the world. The girl, now an old woman, warns of venturing into the forests after twilight.

"The green lets them hide in plain sight, their steps one with nature and their desire for food unending." When pressed about what food, she grimaced and looked away.

"Kidneys."

www.facebook.com/tjayleawriter
Twitter: @tjaylea

THE BLOOD ACCORD
NICK MOORE

Marco's legs shook as he crouched behind the boulder. His tormentors, shouting threats, drew closer.

Marco could not know that millenia before men had trapped something dark there, this place lost to the wilderness. Bound and cursed, and left to be forgotten.

He closed his eyes and prayed. Blood from his nose dripped down his chin and hit the dirt. Something beneath him spoke, "Blood, and a request for freedom. Speak your desire, set me free."

Marco pointed towards the bullies and heard screams, then silence. He walked out of the forest peacefully, following giant footprints burned into the earth.

www.nmwrites.com.

LABYRINTH

KASE GLIDEWELL

A roar came from the darkness behind Arete as she stumbled and fell to the ground. Her knees scraped on the wet stones, the flame of her candle sputtering out. She pushed herself up and began running blindly in the dark, the cries growing closer.

There had to be a way out of the labyrinth!

Her bare feet slapped the painfully cold ground as she ran. Arete turned a corner, finding herself at a dead end. Tears flowed down her cheeks as she heard the roar right behind her. She squeezed her eyes shut, and turned to face the Minotaur.

DRAUGR
TOR-ANDERS ULVEN

I went fishing with my grandfather in late autumn. A sunny day, not too windy, but when the fog crept in we decided to turn around. I saw her then, on a rocky islet. A pale young girl cradling a bronze urn.

"It's a Draugr," my grandfather warned, "A drowned soul yearning for lost love."

I misread the look in his eyes, mistaking it for fear. He died a week later, and the funeral was lovely. A childhood picture of my late grandmother graced his coffin, and I stumbled back as the realisation hit me.

It was her, the Draugr.

https://www.facebook.com/hyperobscure/
https://www.reddit.com/user/hyperobscura

THE CHORUS OF A SIREN'S SONG

JACLYN FULSCHER

Captain Dillinger stepped away from his crew, leaning over the bow of his ship. His eyes were glazed and his lips parted slightly, his body swaying back and forth to the tune of the sweetest song heard by man.

Immediately she jumped out of the water, her hands cold and boney. They wrapped around his neck, ripping him from the ship. He fell into the black waters, struggling to pull away from her.

She snapped the bones in his wrist and plunged her sharp shark like teeth into his neck, watching life leave his filmy eyes.

She consumed him entirely.

THE DEVIL AND THE DEVIL
ABIRAN RAVEENTHIRAN

It seemed as though walking across the room was barely manageable by this man. Could this fragile creature have accomplished the feats they say he committed?

He had one simple question that would determine the man's true self. "Tell me, human. What drove you to commit the atrocities you did?" Yama questioned the mortal.

A smirk grew on the man's face, exposing his yellowed and missing teeth. A few strands of white hair fell in front of his face, and through them two malevolent eyes burned hotter than inextinguishable Hell-fire. The malevolent gaze, so hate-filled, ceased the doubt within Yama.

https://www.goodreads.com/author/show/
18247229.Abiran_Raveenthiran
https://www.instagram.com/lightweaversreads/r
https://twitter.com/AbiranRavi

Sins of the Father

Chris Hewitt

"**H**elp me!"

He pleaded, his voice reverberating around the ravine.

"Help me."

She echoed mockingly, gazing down at his broken body.

The pain was unbearable.

"You did this!"

She dropped the severed rope, shaking her head.

"You did this."

"Why?"

"Why!"

Her eyes flashed, but she had no words. Hera had seen to that, and Zeus had remained silent. He would pay for that, a distant commotion giving her captive a promise of salvation.

"Thank the gods! Help!"

Echo thrust her hands over his mouth. It was her turn to remain silent, and Zeus' bastard son would not be found.

Twitter: @i_mused_blog
Blog: http://mused.blog/

LEVIATHAN
Henry Herz

The ship was jeered, the harbour cleared,
Grimly did we sail.
Beneath the skies, across the waves
To hunt the fearsome whale.
Down dropt the breeze, the sails fell slack,
We drifted on the sea.
And we did speak only to break
The silence of the sea!
But then Leviathan came,
So perilous and strong.
He struck with his o'erpowering flukes,
And battered us south along.
We limped away with a shattered prow,
The beast pursued with furrowed brow.
It rammed us again, hunters now prey.
I gazed upon the broken deck
And saw where all the dead men lay.

Tsukumogami

Gabriella Balcom

"Dump that nasty, ancient thing." Suki said, watching her servants toss it outside.

Her father had insisted on keeping the old table, passed down through generations, but he'd died yesterday.

"Tsukumogami!" the servants shrieked, referring to living objects becoming angry after being discarded. They dashed away.

Standing on two legs the table charged Suki, a face glaring from its underside.

She fled, screaming.

The creature pounced, stomping her body before picking it up and repeatedly slamming it to the ground.

Blood bubbled from Suki's lips.

Smashing her head flat with one leg the table retreated, strutting back into its home.

THE MAYAN WHO LAUGHED
ANDREW ANDERSON

Camazotz stood menacingly before the bloodied figure hung upon the wall of the temple. It was Balam-Quitze — the Jaguar with the Sweet Smile — who had poisoned the waters of the Cenote, killing hundreds of innocent villagers.

Despite the rough interrogation thus far, he was still grinning at Camazotz, silently taunting him. The priest Aapo shouted from outside, "Master Camazotz, you must be hungry. I could bring you some atole, perhaps?"

Camazotz grinned and turned back to his prisoner, his fangs glinting in the torchlight.

"No Aapo, I think I'll be okay for now."

The smile finally fell from Balam-Quitze's face.

Twitter: @soorploom

THE ACOLYTE
SARAH MATTHEWS

"Jubilation be upon you, my acolyte," whispered Celaeno Mysichore. "Now touch my robes, and I shall receive you."

The acolyte touched the white marble folds and watched in awe as obsidian tendrils spiraled outward from her touch, enveloping the carven form of her beloved patron. The darkness flowed up over Her outstretched arms, Her delicate antlers, Her predatory smile.

As the deity stepped gracefully from Her plinth, the birch trees that ringed Jubilation Grove trembled at Her splendor. Wails of praise echoed through the grove.

Celaeno Mysichore descended upon Her acolyte, and the ancient steps of The Dance began anew.

Twitter @superbfinch.

WOODLAND MANAGEMENT
EMMA K. LEADLEY

The woodsman was new to his employment, though experienced in his craft. He started his first morning chopping down unruly saplings, pausing whenever his axe fell.

Each time the wind whistled harder, and the leaves rustled louder. When he stopped to wipe sweat from his brow he thought to eat lunch under a nearby oak. Nestling back against the ancient trunk he slept soundly in the midday sun, not feeling the trees moving and or hearing the chorus of creaks.

He awoke to roots binding his limbs, the leaves and earth rising to meet him. "No more," whispered the forest.

www.emmaleadley.co.uk
www.twitter.com/autoerraticism

THE SKOGSRÅ'S TAIL

JEN CHICHESTER

Ingvar was speechless.

Emerald eyes peered at him from beneath a wild mop of sun-glazed auburn hair.

"Let me show you the way out of these woods," she spoke in a low, lullaby-esque voice. "Take my hand."

Without thought he put his dirt-smeared hand into her dainty, pristine one. She offered him a coy smile as her fingers tightened around his. Even if he wanted to let go he could not. Her talon-like nails dug their way into his skin.

From beneath her billowing, white skirt emerged a cow's tail. Little did Ingvar know he had stumbled upon a skogsrå.

www.facebook.com/JenChichesterWritesStuff/
Instagram: @hopelesspierrot

THE SPRIGGAN
T.J. LEA

No matter what they say, this isn't my daughter. It never was, something snatched her. A grotesque miniature frame of brittle bones, leathery skin and bulging eyes sunken into an ancient skull with wispy hair and gnarled teeth curled into a sick smile. The Spriggan has been in Cornwall for an eon, and it set its yellowed eyes on my daughter, leaving this deformed changeling in her place. They say she was always this way, but I know why they turn a blind eye: they have children of their own that may be snatched away, if they offend the Spriggan.

www.facebook.com/tjayleawriter
Twitter: @tjaylea

La Viuda del Árbol
Joel R. Hunt

Martin had lost his patience. This project was costing thousands every day, and a single protester was holding up the operation. His superstitious workers refused to cut down the forest after seeing her, claiming she was some spirit of the forest; 'La Viuda del Árbol'.

Now Martin was striding through the trees, ready to flush her out himself.

A soft patch of ground suddenly gave way. Martin tumbled down into a crevice in the rocks below, his leg jamming between two stones. He looked up to see a smiling old lady, vines growing across the gap to seal him inside.

https://twitter.com/JoelRHunt1
https://www.reddit.com/r/JRHEvilInc/

Jake's Visit to India

Gabriella Balcom

"Only idiots believe in make-believe gods," fifteen-year-old Jake muttered, staring at the statue mostly obscured by trees. He'd wandered off while his family visited tourist sites.

Grabbing a branch, he began hitting the statue before pelting it with stones.

"That represents Shiva," an Indian man said, walking toward the teen.

"It's stupid."

The man's body shimmered, rapidly growing larger. "I'm Shiva," he boomed, eyes blazing. Snatching up vines he whipped Jake, ignoring his shrieks, then beat him with a tree limb.

Soon bloody flesh and bones lay everywhere.

"Only idiots ridicule gods," Shiva said before vanishing.

https://m.facebook.com/GabriellaBalcom.lonestarauthor

To Drop Thy Sword

Steve Stred

Grasping the thick, leather book in one hand he felt its power surge through his skin, up his arm and deep into his soul.

He'd long heard of this tome, written by the ancient ones. Within it foretold of the man who'd possess it and change the course of a war.

Far below, where the battle raged on, his men were boxed in.

They'd be slaughtered shortly.

The Knight dropped his sword, opened the book and read the first sentence.

A powerful percussion blasted forth from the ink, knocking him back.

On the battlefield the enemy fell, lifeless and defeated.

www.stevestredauthor.wordpress.com
www.amazon.com/author/stevestred

THE NIGHT MARE
AMBER M. SIMPSON

The mare slid through the keyhole, a mist of black and gray. Hovering between the door and bed she slowly solidified into her nightly visage: beautiful, dark, and dreadful.

She snickered at the broom and shoes turned inwards beside the bed, the man's foolish attempts at warding her off.

Graceful as a cat she leaped on his chest, gazing into his sleeping face. His eyelids twitched frantically, and he moaned as his dreams grew dark and sinister.

The mare smiled as she crouched atop the man's trembling body, eagerly imagining all the wonderful terrors she would inflict upon his dreams.

https://ambermsimpson.com/
https://www.facebook.com/authorambermsimpson/

THE SLAUGHS
PAUL BENKENDORFER

They lurk in the darkness. Slaughs, wraiths, souls of the damned searching for others to join their coven.

I can hear them, howling from throats filled with a thousand dying screams.

Then I see them in the fog. Silver figures shrouded in a veil of white mist, cloaked in the curtain of night. Their crimson eyes burn like millions of tiny pyres, and their wails grow louder.

My dying grandfather knows they've come for him as he waits in bed. Their wails become deafening, their phantom arms reaching for him.

I slam the shutters closed, but there's too much silence.

https://twitter.com/PBenkendorfer

IGNORANCE
CHRIS BANNOR

When their young men began to disappear, those searching the newly discovered cavern, his people recalled tales long since forgotten.

He ignored them all.

An earthquake had uncovered a long-buried cavern, and he wanted to be the first to see inside, to explore the beauties that nature had hidden.

What he found was death.

The creature had a long neck, with curled horns adorning its head. Its teeth were bared as it glided through the lake's waters, and he froze in terror at its speed.

A single word dripping from his lips as the beast reared back to strike.

"Ogopogo."

Facebook: @chrisbannorauthor
www.ChrisBannor.com

Scylla

Timothy Friesenhahn

Their ship had already been capsized, screaming sailors swimming away furiously.

The beast was too quick, and the waves it created threw them into the air.

If they were lucky they smashed back into the water, but most of the screaming men were flung directly into one of the beasts six mouths. The six headed sea-dragon destroyed all who sailed her channel.

The surviving sailors begged for mercy, but the ones she didn't eat were subjected to a more sinister fate. Thrown upon her cliff they would be prisoner to her natural form, spending eternity as slaves to her desires.

Sword of Freyr
Andrew Anderson

Freyr, seeking water, had wandered into the wrong town.

"Pretty boy, with a nice blade too," jeered the elder, whose armed townsfolk menacingly surrounded the stranger. Emboldened by the strength in numbers, the elder snatched for Freyr's sword.

This weapon would only fight if its wielder was wise, and it fell from the unworthy man's hand. He shrugged, instead stabbing Freyr in the gut with his dagger.

Freyr fell to the ground, close to death.

"Fool, don't you realise who I am? Your harvest, your wealth...gone…Sverthaust…"

The sword Sverthaust obeyed, rising up and slaughtering the bloodthirsty, unworthy town.

AWAKENING TIDE

THOMAS WAKE

The tide goes in and out, almost pacing their steps along the bottom of the sea. The thick, endless mist covers the small, seaside town like a mortician covering a cadaver. People slumber, blissfully unaware of the ancient curse creeping along their streets and houses.

Pale moonlight filters through the mist, a beacon to the maritime dead now dragging their dripping feet on the cobblestone. A nefarious promise, made by the forefathers, finally gets fulfilled. Doors splinter, windows shatter and a thousand screams pierce the night. And, in the golden dawn, there is only the lingering stench of the draugr.

https://twitter.com/ThomasWake12

The Final Journey

Kathleen Halecki

Sustained on the long, dark journey by the kipsum ritual performed every morning, she could still hear her parent's teary voices praying.

Clutching the gold coins tightly in her pocket she patiently waits on the shores of the Hubur River, ignoring those around her rending their garments in their anguish. With no money to pay the stone-faced ferryman, Urshanabi, they are pushed aside, their pleas ignored as they attempt to rush aboard.

The wails become louder echoing over the passengers as the ferry glides across the water. She turns away helplessly as the forgotten dead are left on the shores.

PRAYERS
S. C. MORGAN

The family kneeled before the crude altar, praying to their deity. Times were difficult: crops were marred by blight, and blistering heat forced them beyond their fields for the bare necessities.

Papa extended his arms towards the altar, his head bowed solemnly. His son mimicked these motions, bringing a tired smile to Mama's face.

The candle light sputtered as a cloaked figure appeared from the shadows. Mama's smile grew larger with relief: their savior had finally arrived. Her smile vanished as he emerged from the shadows wearing a too-wide, jagged grin.

Her screams echoed their final deliverance through the trees.

www.facebook.com/SCMorganAuthor/
Twitter: @ScmorganAuthor

Crops and Fire
Al-Hazred

Drums and flutes echoed across the temple, muffling the voices of Gades' citizens. A fire in the center of the room projected dancing shadows unto their faces. One of the men comforted a crying woman.

"Crops will be good."

Around the fire lay seven cribs, the cries of the infants made inaudible by the instruments.

Out of the shadows emerged a vaguely human shape, flapping nostrils and protruding yellow eyes moving in frenzy. The ram-headed being emitted a guttural roar, showing rows of malformed fangs before proceeding to feast.

The drums kept growing louder as Melqart consumed its innocent sacrifice.

MARŌN

N.M. BROWN

Screams billow through the corridor, blasting us out of a peaceful sleep.

"Tor, Lori's having nightmares again." I grumble, nudging my husband. "You go this time."

"She always wants both of us." He warns.

A blast of cold air penetrates my bones as we enter her bedroom. The ethereal figure of a monkey sits on Lori's chest, its hands squeezing her throat.

"It's a Mare!" Tor shouted as he lunged forward. The monkey changes shape as it disappears.

Lori's hair is so tangled that we cut it. Silver strands always grow back, a piece of her soul forever lost.

THE VOICES IN YOUR HEAD ARE AFRAID

KAREN HESLOP

No, not of you, don't be silly. They're afraid of the things that lurk in the corners, slippery and liquid like oil. That sharp, creeping dread you feel when you're awake? It's the remnants of the torture the voices endure while you sleep. Didn't you wonder why they shriek and dredge up horrifying memories at night?

The ancient gods that cling to life's waning fragments need a host. They love that they can obliterate and replace your friends, so go ahead and take that pill. Enjoy your rest, but bear this in mind as you drift off: I'm not George.

Twitter: @kheslopwrites

THE TRICKSTER

CALLUM PEARCE

The trickster god watched the earth, dreaming of mischief and mayhem. He loved to disguise himself as some innocent thing, then create havoc for his own amusement. Spying a wedding at one of his churches, an evil grin cracked his face.

A wicked plan was forming.

Hurtling toward Earth he chose the shape of a pig. What fun he would have running wild in the aisles! He noticed the fire and the spit too late, ignorant of the man with the knife approaching.

That evening, unaware, the happy guests enjoyed their roasted meat with one less god to worry about.

https://mobile.twitter.com/Aladdinsane79
https://m.facebook.com/calmpeace13/

Beaten To The Punch
Melody Grace

"Hangman, Hangman, let my soul be free. Take me to the underground for all eternity."

I watched in fascination as the group began to quickly tie a noose around the girl's neck, finalizing the ancient ritual as she giggled.

Then I heard his steps in the distance, and knew I had to act fast. With a swift wave of my hand the rope snapped her neck. Screams filled the night just before The Hangman stepped into the clearing.

"Seriously, Death, another one? This isn't a competition, asshole..." He shook his head as I grinned back in silence.

It was now.

https://www.facebook.com/nocturnalnanny/
https://www.twitter.com/nocturnalnanny/

Black Goat of the Woods
K.T. Tate

I just wanted a baby. All medicine had failed, I'd stopped caring who answers my prayers. Desperation felt like courage at the ancient fertility site.

Drums echoed through the forest, words unknown pulled me like a siren's call. Dragging my husband we joined the dancers, naked and brazen. Frenzy took over as the stars blot out, trees revealing unearthly hooves.

She manifests.

I raised my dagger, sacrificing all I love for all I want. Blood spilled. Raised up, supported by great claws, I screamed as she made me whole.

Awakening I find my soul is empty, but not my body.

https://eldritch-hollow.com/

WISHING TREE
JOE SCIPIONE

Katie stood at the stump of her beloved wishing tree and cried. The tree was magic, it had given her everything she wished for, but then her mom called the 'tree men' to remove the old, leafless tree from their yard.

"You don't know what it does!" Katie shouted at her mom as she ran out of the house to the spot where her tree once stood, where twisted branches once filled the sky. "How could you do this!?"

Katie wept for the tree that had granted her desires, glaring back towards her mom.

"I wish she was dead."

Twitter @JoeScipione0
Instagram: JoeScipione0

Rod of Fire
Sean P. Chatterton

Alexandros stood before the ancient ruins of the Hall of Worlds, the Rod of Fire clenched tightly in his hand. Before him stood the doorways to infinite worlds, each unknown and uncharted. Behind him was his relentless nemesis, the destroyer of his kind.

Alexandros had to choose how to save his people: Turn back and fight his enemy, or step forward into an unknown future.

Mooncoyn, the tribe's seer, had told him that his fate was already decided.

"Each great journey starts with a single step," she had whispered.

So, with a little trepidation, Alexandros walked through the first doorway.

http://www.seanpchatterton.co.uk
https://www.facebook.com/sean.p.chatterton

TITANOMACHY

Zoey Xolton

Zeus met in secret with his brother Hades, and spoke with him at length into the night. At dawn the following day an almighty quake shook the earth as Hades unlocked the ancient gates of Tartarus, unleashing a legion of cyclops and the three dreaded Hekatonkheires — the fifty-headed, one-hundred-handed giants.

Zeus lit the sky with glorious thunderbolts as the children of Gaia marched forth upon the enemies of the Olympians, the old gods — the Titans. For ten years they had battled, and now the tide of war was finally turning!

Soon Zeus would be the undisputed King of the Gods.

www.zoeyxolton.com

THE DEATH OF BAAL
MATT LUCAS

Hundreds pled for Baal to ignite their offering. In one act he could rekindle their faith, and destroy Elijah's inferior deity. The oxen-headed god reached from the clouds towards their altar.

Baal trembled as he summoned his full might, yet not even an ember answered his followers' prayers. Across the field Elijah raised his hand skyward. A pillar of fire struck the prophet's altar.

A blazing river branched from the pillar and consumed Baal. The impotent deity fell to his knees as holy fire scorched his flesh. As his body crumbled to ash Baal knew the source of true power.

https://twitter.com/MattDLuke
https://www.instagram.com/mattdluke/?hl=en

RIDERS IN THE NIGHT
HOLLEY CORNETTO

Ear-splitting shrieks and the thundering of ghastly hooves filled the wood, a dark symphony to herald their coming. The rider at the helm was magnificent, his eyes glowing bright like Hellfire. As the riders closed in around me I raised my knife, sinking it deep within my chest. My mouth filled with the metallic taste of blood.

All was darkness, all was lost as I was swallowed by oblivion. When I opened my eyes again the Erl-King stood before me, offering me the reins of a nightmarish steed. "Welcome to the Wild Hunt."

At last, finally, I had found them.

My Fifteen Minutes
Jennifer Winters

I'm a celebrity, I think as the locals meet me with cheers.

"So, you saw him!" the mayor says, elated.

A collective cheer, and a then a voice: "Tell us!"

I describe myself on the backwoods road, lost and without a phone. I tell of the towering shadow emerging from the trees. Of the horns and eyes.

Several handshakes and selfies later, the mayor takes my hand, squeezing.

"After generations of patient waiting and worship, he returns! And for the blood that will welcome him . . ."

Her grip tightens. ". . . he has provided a lamb."

Twitter @wordywinters

Demeter's Anguish
DeBickel

Wind against rocky coasts, weeds growing around aging domiciles. Autumn in Greece arrived as it pleased, though the calendar marked the day Persephone left with Hades for the Underworld.

The inhabitants of Navagio don't need a calendar, all they need is to feel the waters, and to hear the siren's screams. Shrieking, piercing, unworldly howling, far removed from the musical notes that would grace summer nights.

"Gran," Phoebe asked as they neared the coast one morning, "why do they scream?"

"Demeter cursed them, engoní. They did not stop Hades from abducting Persephone, so now they must feel her broken heart."

THE STAG
HUNTER LaCROSS

The stag meanders through the algid moonlit night, protecting the creatures of his forest. I, the hunter, can see through his clever facade. Cernunnos is the deity of this forest, no mere deer, and as he passes me I stare fixedly upon him.

I pray he won't notice me, but that is in vain. Will the deity of the forest bring forth my final breathe?

Crunch after crunch resounds as he approaches me, until my gun's desperate bang echoes around us. He regards me with ancient eyes, their disapproving glint obvious.

I will leave the woods in peace, for now.

Reddit: U/XxAtroticusxX

FLEE
STEVE STRED

The Hell hounds brayed and howled behind him as he rushed deeper and deeper into the woods. What lived in the depths of the forest was infinitely worse than what chased him, but he had no other choice. Run, or be slaughtered.

As his feet pounded the moss and splashed in the collected puddles, he saw motion in the distance before him.

He could hear the beasts gaining on him, their breathing becoming louder and louder.

His blood ran cold when he saw the wraith step from behind a tree a dozen meters ahead.

Their jaws closed over his head.

www.stevestredauthor.wordpress.com
www.amazon.com/author/stevestred

A Sleeping Serpent
Clint Foster

One deep breath and I leap, jumping the ten feet across the threshold in a bound. My eyes are fixed on the mirrored shield before me. I know my fate if they stray, and the statues that grope at their eyes all around me bear testament to their failures in the past. Nimble as a cloud I wander the gorgon's nest, and I keep my sharp sword clutched at my side. It happens in a second, a frantic instant, a hiss. My blade cleaves her snaked head from her shoulders. I breathe, and I smile, for Medusa haunts no longer.

www.facebook.com/clintfosterauthor

OFFERINGS

BRIAN ROSENBERGER

The sea provided the village with many things. The air was fresher, the sound of the waves soothed people to sleep.

The sea provided sustenance – lobsters, shrimps, crabs, scallops, fish. It was only fitting they fed the sea in return, as the villagers were grateful for all the sea provided.

The sacrifice was more than tradition, it was their way of giving thanks, but this sacrifice was found wanting. The drowned children floated to shore, rejected.

The God beneath the Waves must be appeased.

Tomorrow would be another sacrifice, but tonight the sound of the waves soothed no one.

https://www.facebook.com/HeWhoSuffers
https://www.instagram.com/brianrosenberger7097

CERBERUS

S. C. MORGAN

Leonora crawled through the trees, holding the swaddled baby tightly against her. Smoke from the remnants of her village filled the air, stinging her eyes and forcing her to take shallow breaths. Glancing back through the smoky haze, praying they had escaped, she noticed a hulking shape moving towards them.

As she stepped between two trees a branch snapped behind her, stopping Leonora where she stood. Turning she stumbled on an exposed root, sending her to the forest floor. The beast's three heads growled, as if from one. Looking into its eyes a single name burned in her mind: Cerberus.

www.facebook.com/SCMorganAuthor/
Twitter: @ScmorganAuthor

THE MISKATONIC MADNESS
MARK ANTHONY SMITH

"**W**hat is that author called, the one who wrote about the Old Ones? He wrote 'Dagon'."

The University librarian's brow furrowed as it clouded over outside. He glanced out the window at the darkening sky, the weight of sleepless nights were carried in his face.

He leaned over.

"Sir, that author is H.P. Lovecraft, and you must act fast!" I leaned back and appraised the stark terror in his eyes. He was bordering on madness. It was as if something from another dimension was colouring his frenzied mind. As the clouds gathered his soul stood testament that Cthulhu will return.

Twitter: @MarkAnthonySm16
Facebook: Mark Anthony Smith- Author

OF LOVE, OF ICHOR
NOA COVO

They think she was born of sea spray and golden sunlight. Aphrodite of beauty, of love, of future promises.

Mortals and gods flock her, trying to grasp her divinity, bathing in her radiance. Aphrodite lets them draw closer.

She remembers her birth: the ichor, the gore.

She lets them draw closer, and her glow intensifies. She smiles as they attempt to reach her, possess her.

Aphrodite lets them try. She knows exactly what she's made of, the pain and betrayal and curses. She is the consequence of the first murder in creation.

She knows she can make them all burn.

Twitter @covo_noa

Love Me, Love My Cat
K.T. Tate

You really should stop screaming. Call me a witch all you want, but I prefer priestess. You see, dearest, I saw you. I saw you kicking Tiger. We don't just respect cats in this house, we worship them.

I did mention it.

Let me explain: This is a summoning circle, and that monstrous shadow of grace and sleek velvet is Bastet, Goddess of cats. A razor clawed, obsidian nightmare predator. Not as pretty, or human, as the ancient Egyptian artwork, but I love her and her children.

You hurt us, so you really should run.

Cats prefer hunting their prey.

https://eldritch-hollow.com/

A Promise Made is a Promise Kept

Andra Dill

Medeina followed the she-wolf. A young wolf whined, bumping Medeina's hand with his dark head and licking nervously at her fingers. The groans and wails emanating from her beloved woods soon had the Goddess flying ahead of the pack.

Where thick-trunked walnut and oak had once stood tall, only their bleeding stumps remained. The stench of toiling men permeated the air. Grief pierced Medeina. The mourning trees shuddered, beseeching her for vengeance.

These humans had forgotten the old ways, the promises made long ago. Time to remind them.

A gnawing, wild hunger assailed Medeina.

"Their blood will atone," she vowed.

www.facebook.com/andradillauthor
https://twitter.com/aedill

NØKKEN

TOR-ANDERS ULVEN

Deep within the forest there's a lovely pond surrounded by majestic pine trees. Sometimes I'll sit down with my fiddle and play a soft tune, the natural acoustic carrying the sound for miles. Sooner or later they will appear. Sometimes a hunter, sometimes a fisherman. They will applaud me, sit down, and tell me the tale of Nøkken.

"Did you know," they'll say, "That Nøkken would play its fiddle to lure wanderers into the murky depths?"

I'll nod and smile. "Of course I know."

Then I'll drag them screaming with me into the awaiting eternal embrace of my dark home.

https://www.facebook.com/hyperobscure/
https://www.reddit.com/user/hyperobscura

BABY DOLL

LAURENCE SULLIVAN

Ayaka kneeled on her tatami mat as she chanted away, cutting each paper doll down to size as her calls for protection grew more frantic.

These little katashiro would soon form her only defence. Each would have to be ready to receive part of the curse she knew would be incoming imminently, so she needed to work faster.

Ayaka had never meant to hurt her baby. The curse wouldn't care; it would come for her regardless.

Her tears only making the spell more indistinct, deep down Ayaka knew that hanging even a hundred around her home couldn't save her now…

www.laurencesullivan.co.uk
Twitter @LozzySullivan

DEAD FISH
RUSSELL SMEATON

She could smell the fish a long way off. The stench of decay mingled with sea-salt, bringing back memories of childhood holidays. Seagulls took flight, squawking their displeasure at her approach.

As far as the eye could see the beach was littered with dead fish. Buzzing flies created a hazy cloud, tears pricked her eyes and thickening her throat at the sight of the wreckage.

In the distance the cloud of flies solidified, becoming both mountainous and humanoid. Her tears dried, and a smile broke her frown.

The summoning had worked.

She waded into the sea to meet her daemon.

https://www.facebook.com/tikirussy/
www.amazon.co.uk/Russell-Smeaton/e/B06XSYJ8TP

CYCLOPS
ANN WYCOFF

Thirty men shipwrecked on *my* island. I let them share my cave, then what? Those ingrates drove a burning stake into *my* eye while I slept!

Sure, I'm a giant, but I've only got one eye.

I'm subject to their cruel games, their favorite of which is to encircle me and jab me with barbed spears.

"Dance!"

"Caper!"

My logic and rage run a race, with my life as the stakes.

Jest, laugh, play the buffoon, or rage, strike and kill?

Soon enough the joke will be on them, for when a cyclops loses her eye it quickly grows back.

Blue Bandana

C. Marry Hultman

"What do you want from me?" He stammered.

"Harry," Xochiquetzal smiled, her voice barely audible over the Dia De Los Muertos celebrations outside. "You know exactly why I'm here. I have chased you from port to port. Someone must protect my girls."

She indicated the bloody remains of his latest victim tied up beside him. He strained against the blue bandana binding his wrists. Xochiquetzal sauntered towards him, pointed red nails gliding up his naked leg. She climbed upon him.

"And you believed I wouldn't find you."

Placing a marigold in his mouth she slid her blade between his ribs.

https://wisconsinnoir.wixsite.com/wi

A Death Overdue

Matthew A. Clarke

Francis Gillingham had lived many lives, had many names, buried countless lovers and children. The one constant in his life: his yearly trip to the Escambray mountains of Cuba.

Francis had a secret. He'd discovered the Fountain of Youth after the Spanish invasion, and collapsed the cave that housed it.

Now, reaching the leafy crag, he was desperate for a taste of the elixir, and he could feel his body rotting.

But the entrance stood open, excavated. The fountain was gone.

Francis screamed as skin and flesh fell from his frame.

Vultures circled, hearing his cries. They'd eat well tonight.

www.facebook.com/fotc87

LONELY
HEIDI ANN WILLITS

I held my face in my hands, trying to drown the dull, constant hissing sound in my ears. It never went away. Through the white noise I heard loud creaking, splashing and yelling.

Darting from my cave, eyes straining and squinting in the light, I was delighted to find my meal had arrived. They scattered in all directions, some turning to stone if they met my eyes.

It was like cat-and-mouse, I had to pounce before they looked at me. Finally, I cornered my prey. I hunted, then I bit down. My head of snakes ripped him to shreds with me.

https://twitter.com/heidiwillits
https://www.facebook.com/Heidi-Ann-Willits-100217031460654/

HUNTER OF THE CORRUPT
ANDY LEAVY

I lay on the Avondale Forest floor, blood pouring from an open wound in my chest. Above me stands Bás Sciathánach, its boned wings beating in the night air. My friends' blood is painted across its talons and featureless face, needled teeth stained with crimson.

It took us out with ease, razor-sharp claws tearing through us like butter. It came for us, for Bálor willed it. Its lack of eyes hindering it little, it could smell the darkness of our souls. We sealed our destiny with our corrupt acts. We believed ourselves more powerful than fate, but fate has arrived.

Twitter: @midniteauth0r
https://www.facebook.com/LeavyWriting/

Corn Festival
Al Provance

Gregory's tears spattered onto his blood soaked hands, leaving rivulets in their wake as they dripped onto the viscera-covered floor.

This job was hard, but necessary, and only his family carried on the tradition. The Corn Festival drew curious visitors from the cities a few hours away, and if just one tourist went missing there wouldn't be an investigation.

The Corn Maiden thirsted beneath the ground. She sent her children up through the soil, just to have their bodies eaten and their flesh ripped away. Gregory wondered if the Corn Maiden cried as he did, yet he made another incision.

https://www.facebook.com/Al-Provance
https://twitter.com/somrael

I AM

Stacey Jaine McIntosh

I am the daughter of a King who forgot my name, I am the daughter of a Queen who never saw my face.

I am here, I am ready, and I will rule. The day will come when everyone will know who I am!

The day will come when they will shout my name in triumph. I will lead them to victory, and they will bow down to me in reverence and gratitude.

I will give them purpose, because without purpose they are nothing.

I am everything. I am the light, and the darkness.

I am Ammit, Devourer of souls.

www.staceyjainemcintosh.com

THE SKUGGABALDUR

CHRIS HEWITT

The hunter threw the sack on the table. "There's ya thief. Now get me a drink!" The inn fell quiet.

"What's that?" the farmer asked.

"A fox. A cat," the hunter gasped, between swigs of ale. "Who cares? Where's my money?"

Panic spread through the room, a jug tumbling from the barmaid's hand.

"Look for ya self," the hunter said, throwing open the bag. Before anyone could react the beast leapt free, the villagers falling one-by-one to its angry, cursed gaze.

All but the barmaid, for she hid.

Her grandmother's story of the Skuggabaldur was no longer a tall tale.

Twitter: @i_mused_blog

Ragnarök

Sandy Butchers

Blood trickled down from razor-like fangs, and a loud snarl cut through the horrid silence.

The sun cowered before the foaming wolf, as this was the moment that the vile creature would shred it to pieces.

The wolf paced closer. It had already filled its gut with the moon, but the sight of the sun had made it hungry for more. It knew that, with a snap of its jaws, it would unleash the bloody mayhem that had been foretold by the ancient prophets. It knew that, with a tear of its fangs, the end of the Gods would begin.

http://www.sandybutchers.com
https://www.facebook.com/AuthorSandyButchers/

Drumming Of My Heart
Michelle River

My hand trembled against the cold shield as I listened intently within the garden of stone. There was no sound, except the constant drumming of my heart.

For days I waited for Calem's valiant return with the monster's severed head, but he didn't emerge.

The monster still lives, and only I am left.

I launched forward, sword held high in my iron grip, the mane of serpents hissing at my approach. Her scarlet gaze burned into my soul, holding fast my feet upon the ground where they fell.

My scream locked within my lungs as the burning stone encased me.

www.facebook.com/michelleriverauthor/
www.twitter.com/MRiver_Writes

Fateful Coin

Michael D. Nadeau

If I'd known who owned the coin when I found it I would've thrown it back in the stream.

The tarnished gold coin, grime-covered and wet, was warm to the touch. It had ancient markings in a language I didn't understand, and little did I know the horror touching it would summon.

The creature was tenacious, never giving up, and had wounded me badly. He was very short, and dressed in old clothes with a raggedy hat. His red beard was covered in my blood.

His cry was always the same: The thief must die!

Who knew Leprechauns were real?

https://karsisthebard.wordpress.com/

From Clay

Willem V. Much

The Spring of Sorrows loved new arrivals. Freshly disembodied souls always pressed close to her scaly hide, whispering ceaselessly. This one begged for eyesight, that one wanted genitals that would put a stallion to shame.

Some wished to never die again, others wished to live again. The Spring of Sorrows granted every request, and smiled when the fools thanked her. Those unlucky souls that returned to her pit for a second time never praised her when they woke up.

They learned that, of all the demons in the Underworld, the one that gave them their flesh back was the cruelest.

https://twitter.com/VeryScholar

CURSE OF THE KODAMA
JEN CHICHESTER

I tried to warn him.

Baka gaijin.

The ax sliced through the protective layer of dead bark, but instead of sap a dark, crimson substance oozed forth.

Kodama.

He hacked again, and again, and again. Blood splattered his face and torso.

"What's wrong, Kenichi?" he asked. "It's just a little sap!" He raised the ax once more.

I opened my mouth, but the "No!" I wanted to shout caught in my throat.

A bright, white orb burst from the tree's core, flying directly into his solar plexus. His eyes glazed over, and the curse would slowly eat away at his soul.

www.facebook.com/JenChichesterWritesStuff/
Instagram: @hopelesspierrot

Twenty-One Candles
Dickon Springate

And then there was one.

One final, black candle whose wax was almost spent, the only thing left illuminating the protective pentagram that barred the slavering abomination from reaching and feasting upon her flesh.

There was no doubt in her mind that she had enunciated the incantation correctly, but the scribbles in the notebook gave no clue as to why it had failed to banish what it had previously summoned.

Had she known of the details surrounding the bloody demise of the original scribe then she would never have chosen to recreate that particular ritual, especially on a new moon.

THE KRAKEN'S CALL

JOSH HERZ

The sea is angry tonight.

The tide is full, the moon glows pale.

Upon the straits along the coast the light

Gleams and is gone.

Beware! It approaches. Foul is the night air!

Listen to the grating roar

Of the ravenous kraken rising from the depths.

The crushing of wood, the drowning of sailors.

The waves draw back flotsam and fling,

At their return, up the high strand.

Begin, and cease, and then again begin.

With tremulous cadence slow, and bring

The renewed stench of death in.

Its feasting done, now I only hear

The kraken's melancholy, long, withdrawing roar.

Cash Grab

Matthew A. Clarke

They said I'd never get this far; they were wrong.

They said I was crazy, but would a crazy person be able pass the trials that have defeated so many men before me? Perhaps.

The rickety suspension bridge is buffeted by wind as I cross the cave. I know I should be wary of footing, but my eyes are fixated on the relic ahead, flanked by tremendous golden statues of the Gods.

Finally, I reach it. It feels warm against my skin.

I fail to lift it, but that's expected.

Imagine what the public will pay to see Thor's hammer!

www.facebook.com/fotc87

Guardians of Memory
Kimberly Rei

A child twisted in his bed, legs pumping as he ran through nightmares.

An old woman sighed, pulling her blankets closer. Her heart ached for days and people she could not recall.

A dog whimpered nearby, sniffing his humans' fears but helpless to act.

Inky shapes moved through the house, slipping from dream to dream. They were known to scholars of the arcane as the Guardians of Memory. A kind name, barely accurate. They stole, these Guardians, taking the good and leaving the sad. They gathered joy, bartering with each other for the finest collection.

Endless, greedy, leaving none untouched.

http://tales.studiorei.org/

BROKEN LYRE
FRED WILLIAMSON

The cave mouth yawned wide, and Helios' light breached the tunnels. For a moment the drab grays and browns of the stone and lichen seemed not so empty, not so forlorn.

The breath of Aeolus' children upon the traveler's cheeks, their wails as they passed him by, and the drip-drop of the subterranean waters reminded him of the song he had played.

A song the world would never again know.

He hugged the broken lyre to his chest, listening to the echoes, but the stone's memory of footsteps recalled only his own. Was he alone? Seeking an answer, Orpheus turned.

FUTAKUCHI-ONNA
DREW STARLING

Eiichi always wondered why his mommy wasn't fat. Every night villagers brought a half-koku of rice to their door, and every morning it was gone. When he asked, mommy smiled sweetly.

"To feed my other mouth, Eiichi-san."

One night Eiichi spied on his mommy's late feasting. Strands of her long, black hair moved on their own, holding dozens of chopsticks while stuffing a snarling second mouth in the back of mommy's head. The mouth had long, sharp teeth and a tongue that was taller than Eiichi.

Suddenly, the movement stopped. Rice dripped from the mouth as it hissed.

"Hungry, Eiichi-san?"

Twitter @ScaryStarling

SONS OF BARK
MARK ANTHONY SMITH

The moon filters through branches to the unlit forest floor. The leaves seethe, brushing against my ankles as the trees mutter that I'm lost. I try to retrace my steps to find the muddy path. I stumble. There are pains as I face the midnight clouds.

They are part of the bark. Those ancient ones peel away from the old tree trunks with their gnarly forms, leaving imprints in the trees where they hid. Their twig hands descend upon me to make the woods a bit more expansive. I scramble to evade the trees, but they take what was me.

Twitter: @MarkAnthonySm16
Facebook: Mark Anthony Smith- Author

THE TROLL BRIDGE

RUSSELL SMEATON

It wasn't our fault, Mum, honest! We only dared Jim to go under the bridge, we didn't force him. You know the bridge, in the middle of the forest? It's really old, choked with rubbish. He crept in, into the dark, and soon we couldn't see him anymore. We called for him, but someone else called back. No, something called back. No-one understood what it said. We waited, and then something shuffled out. It stank, all covered in thick, greasy hair. When it threw Jim's head at us we started screaming. We just ran. It really wasn't our fault.

https://www.facebook.com/tikirussy/
www.amazon.co.uk/Russell-Smeaton/e/B06XSYJ8TP

A Distracting Gift

Galina Trefil

"I'll fill a grave before I marry you," the kidnapped princess declared to the Norseman. So he travelled to Freyja's hall, begging her for a love spell to bind his captive with.

The goddess raised a skeptical golden eyebrow, then gave him a skoggkat kitten. "The girl will keep her word," she warned.

"Then I'll have her before she dies," he scoffed.

When the princess saw the skoggkat, she passionately embraced the warrior. Utterly duped, he never saw her knife until his throat was already slit.

Distantly, Freyja smirked. She was the goddess of love and sex, not of weakness.

https://www.facebook.com/Rabbi-Galina-Trefil-535886443115467/
https://galinatrefil.wordpress.com/

THE BANSHEE'S LAMENT

DAVID A.F. BROWN

After a day of hiking the peaks of Lough Corrib Steve and Becky returned to their guesthouse, a small cottage overseeing a scattering of grassy islands.

The moonlight soon lulled them into a deep slumber, until they heard a noise.

It was a piercing wail, like an animal being skinned alive. Steve grasped Becky's hand, she squeezed back reassuringly. They drifted back to sleep.

Steve awoke to see Becky dangling from the rafters, a bedsheet wrapped around her bowed neck. Her eyes bulged, her mouth gaped. A whisper, through contorted lips, reached him:

We should have heeded the banshee's warning.

www.facebook.com/browndavidaf

The Sword in the Stomach
K. B. Elijah

The boy heaved at the handle, but it didn't budge. He finally gave up, breathless, wearing an ugly scowl.

Yet the girl who followed him gave the barest of tugs, and the weapon came free from the stone. She thrust it into the air to great cheering from the crowd.

The boy tore the sword from her hand and plunged it through her stomach, staining the blade with scarlet.

When he raised the sword they didn't cheer for him, at least not until the wizard at his side gave a small, meaningful cough.

"All hail King Arthur!" the crowd roared.

Twitter: @KBElijah1
Instagram: @k.b.elijah

A Warrior's Call

Steve Stred

He could feel his blood pouring from his stomach, trickling over his hip before it was washed away with the flowing river water.

Looking above he saw the ravens circling like vultures. They'd come to take him soon.

The attack had been brutal, catching the villagers by surprise. He dared not think what they did with his wife and son.

He could hear their horses gallop away, the smell of the huts burning already filling his nostrils.

Would he stay alive long enough to feel the wolves scavenge his flesh?

He closed his eyes, longing to enter the afterlife's halls.

www.stevestredauthor.wordpress.com
www.amazon.com/author/stevestred

THE YULE CAT

CHARLES REIS

With his feet kicking up snow Halldor dashed through a dark forest, his heart throbbing from the snapping of branches that resonated behind him.

A massive, blunt force slammed into his back, sending him tumbling to the ground. He turned his trembling body around.

Staring with its bright-red eyes, a black cat taller than any building lurked above him. It licked its lips and wiggled its whiskers.

As tears fell down his cheek Halldor wished he had received new clothes for Yule to escape this fate, but before he could scream the cat gouged his teeth into the man's body.

www.facebook.com/charles.reis.35
www.instagram.com/cthulhudawn1979/

RISE OF A BEAUTIFUL DAY

XIMENA ESCOBAR

Psamathe's amber eyes squint upon the restless tide, ever higher, ever closer. Swaying, breaking, distracted from her crime of passion. Embedded in the darkest sand, like a secret on the delicious edge of discovery.

Poseidon licks her, teases her, bubbling on her soles. Neither is aware of the silver eyes opening on the ocean floor as Amphitrite's skeletal fist removes Psamathe's dagger from between her ribs.

The sand goddess runs: something is frightening about the incoming wave. But the dagger stuck to the hilt between her shoulder blades crumbles her into a million crystal grains.

Poseidon stills. Sunrise sparkles painfully.

Facebook: @ximenautora

FIREFLIES
RUSSELL SMEATON

Dan and June reached a clearing in the woods, fireflies dancing above their heads. Dan ran off laughing, determined to catch some flies for June.

She smiled and sat down to wait. When he didn't come back she wandered off in the direction he had run. Coming to a beautiful pond, and seeing his clothes by the edge, she understood. Slipping off her clothes and swimming into the middle of the pond was the last thing she did alive.

From murky depths the Nyx pulled June down, excited for two bodies instead of one. The flies and her would feast.

https://www.facebook.com/tikirussy/
www.amazon.co.uk/Russell-Smeaton/e/B06XSYJ8TP

Lilith

Heinrich von Wolfcastle

Her fingers curled around the child's neck. His breath paused, but not his heart. So ripe, so succulent and tasty.

His blood was from the youngest of her first betrothed. A whisper of delight escaped her lips, and in her carelessness she caused the boy to wake.

His father tore into the room, terror palpable at the sight of his bloodied kin. In the dark he pursued the perpetrator to the dancing curtains of the open window, where the moonlight revealed his dream-lover's face.

Before she took flight she kissed his lips, a promise that she would return for him too.

https://www.heinrichvonwolfcastle.com/blog

ECHIDNA
TIMOTHY FRIESENHAHN

From the shadows I saw her slither towards me. The path I tried was too narrow, and I was too dense to realize it.

I was stuck.

Inside the cavity my head peered through a small hole. A goddess from the waist up, a serpent from the waist down, she was at least twelve feet long and three feet around.

My lungs were too constricted to scream.

I watched her face change as her mouth opened to feed. Her goddess-like appearance stretched and twisted, until her giant, snake-like head displayed its huge fangs.

In one bite she'd swallow my head.

www.twitter/@timfriesenhahn
www.facebook.com/timothy.friesenhahn.7

THE DEVIL'S FOOTPRINTS
T.J. LEA

They awakened after heavy snowfall to a sea of unusual hoof prints on rooftops, walls. The locals thought it was the Devil looking for God-fearing souls to torment, but others that night claimed they saw something far worse, something far more concerning.

Black wings, a creature known for breathing blue fire and jumping higher than any being. Oilskin paired with a devilish smile. Of course the locals knew him, for he was already entrenched in legend. The man of diabolical appearance who struck fear into every Englishman, carrying a corpse with ease as he stepped through the snow.

Spring-Heeled Jack.

www.facebook.com/tjayleawriter
Twitter: @tjaylea

THE MORRIGAN
GRANT HINTON

If you manage to find the crones three,
Don't heed their call but turn and flee.
For one with great beauty, hard to deflect,
Will lure out your passion as if unchecked.
The middle one withered and the oldest crone,
Throws out wisdom and knowledge as if it's a bone.
The last one not of this Earthly plain,
Ancient, evil, offers sanctuary from pain.
Be warned, each will take what she deems fair price,
And will leave you lacking when taken thrice.
Your bones will become a part of her cave,
So run now, child, don't be foolish or brave.

https://www.facebook.com/granthintonauthor
https://www.twitter.com/granthinton3

BONES
NOA COVO

Everything returns to the ocean in the end.

The Leviathan's bones are still buried in the sand, waiting. It remembers being crushed, it remembers being eaten by men.

No matter. Meat can regrow, eyes can refill sockets, fins can re-emerge.

It's the bones that matter.

The monstrosity waits for the tide, its bones close to emerging through the sand. Soon it'll be washed away into the water, then it will be reborn.

This time it won't be defeated, and all it needs to do is wait.

After all, everything returns to the ocean in the end.

Twitter @covo_noa

OF BONES AND CORPSES

SANDY BUTCHERS

An anguished voice scraped through the silence when the giant doors opened.

"What do you want, Loki?" The woman in the doorway snapped, when she saw who stood on the path paved with broken skulls.

Loki smiled when he looked at the half rotten face from which his daughter's eyes looked at him. He took her hand, barely more than bones held together by bare sinews. A sigh escaped him when he realized that he must have been the first in centuries to have mastered the road of corpses. "Hella, dear," he answered, "can a father not come to visit?"

http://www.sandybutchers.com
https://www.facebook.com/AuthorSandyButchers/

TALES OF THE MOORLANDS
K.B. ELIJAH

There was a lost dog out on the moors, they said. Dark colour, coiled tail, looked like it was starving.

Leith Maclean spent every second evening searching for it. Those who saw him trailing the moors with a packet of dog biscuits would smile, remembering how he'd taken in a whole nest of baby pigeons last Christmas, and the deer he'd nursed back to health after a hunting incident.

But there was no one out on the night Leith went missing, the howls of the cù-sìth echoing over the lonely moors as it crunched down on his bones and flesh.

Twitter: @KBElijah1
Instagram: @k.b.elijah

The Revenge of Loqi
Jim Bates

The griffin Loqi watched in horror as his beloved Glimpi tumbled through the air to the ground, an arrow through her golden eye. Down below he saw the shooter, a grizzled old shepherd. Loqi quickly gave chase, but the man ran for safety and hid in his caravan.

Loqi circled high above, patiently waiting. Toward sunset the shepherd finally appeared. The griffin attacked, knocking him to the ground and digging his razor-sharp talons deep into the man's chest. Blood streamed in torrents as the human pleaded to be spared.

A vengeance-fueled Loqi didn't care, and began feeding as the man screamed.

www.theviewfromlonglake.wordpress.com

STUPID THING

GABRIELLA BALCOM

Joseph tried to crush the small seps with his foot, but it slithered into nearby brush.

"Stupid thing." He bent, searching for it.

Although the seps resembled an ordinary snake it wasn't; people had learned this the hard way for countless centuries.

It darted forward, squirting venom into Joseph's face.

As the corrosive substance ate away at his skin he screamed, frantically rubbing his cheeks.

Flesh melted from his face in rivulets, revealing bone underneath. Then that, too, began dissolving.

The seps sprayed Joseph again, more of him liquefying until only a puddle of ooze lay on the ground.

https://m.facebook.com/GabriellaBalcom.lonestarauthor

SESHAT
KEVIN J. KENNEDY

They thought she was their scribe. They deemed her a note taker, a record keeper for superior gods. She created the alphabet and writing, yet they demoted her to the consort of Thoth.

She understood the stars, but not only that - she felt them, could read them. She could see the future and had knowledge of the past, as well as a calculative mind.

They underestimated her greatly. Knowledge is true power; wisdom is key, She bided her time. There was no rush, and when the time was right she vanquished the entire pantheon. She was the one true god.

Voodoo Priestess
Kim Plasket

I knew my field of study would lead me into depths unknown, but not to the end my life. I started out researching mystic, ancient Voodoo and its practices, and that was when I met the Hatian Priestess.

She began to send gifts, and when a Voodoo Doll that looked like me arrived I knew it was bad. I woke up one morning filled with dread, and the last thing I saw was the face of the doll held in the hands of the Haitian Priestess.

She smiled as she ripped the doll in half, and me along with it.

PROMETHEUS
MARK KODAMA

The bald-headed vulture circles above. Its darting, soulless eyes forever staring, calculating, evaluating. Its caws, rasping like an ancient dinosaur's, echo against the cliff walls. The scavenger lands on a rock, hungry yet cautious, waiting to rip through my flesh to feast again on my bloodied liver.

I'm helpless. Arms stretched wide, chained to this crag by Zeus, king of the gods, for bringing fire to man. I cannot die, but can fear and feel pain. His putrid breath smells of vomit as his saliva drips onto my open wound.

I am the titan Prometheus, forsaken by man and beast.

Jostedalsrypa

Tor-Anders Ulven

My grandfather always told us we were descended from Jostedalsrypa, the sole survivor of the Black Plague in Jostedalen. The little girl whose fair skin was impossibly untouched by the ravages of the bubonic horror, while the dead lay in piles around her.

"She made a deal," he whispered ominously, "With Pesta herself. A plague in the hearts of her lineage in return for life."

I never believed him, of course. Superstitious nonsense, or so I thought.

I woke up after my heart surgery to a hospital of the dead, bubonic pustules covering the hideous corpses littering the dark hallways.

I Am Ready
Alex Steslow

My ears twitch at the sound of rolling thunder as an unnatural, ichor cloud forms in the sky several miles away.

It aggressively grows, traveling towards me and forcing guests of wind to lift my cloak and rip the hood from my head.

The gods have become angry with me, seeking to exact their vengeance for my betrayal. I stole their strength for my own, rather then returning it as I should have.

Power and light surge through my veins as I wait for their arrival. The gods are furious, and they will strike at me, but I am ready.

CHASED

N.M. BROWN

Ah, men. Neat little creatures, aren't they? I've lured dozens of them into my forest with the smallest hints of affection.

A group of them are walking through the trees, the stupid humans carry torches for light even though the moon's not risen yet.

The largest of them walks over to me. I offer my hand for him to take, batting my eyes provocatively.

He accepts, twirling me aggressively and ripping the back of my dress.

"See?" He booms, yanking my tail. "A Huldra!"

They cheer as the bark on my back catches flame.

I just barely escape their grasp.

GUARDIAN OF TARTARUS
ZOEY XOLTON

"A gift for you, my love," said Hades. The king of the Underworld's smile was a thin, dark line, but there was a gleeful, infernal light that danced behind his ancient, golden eyes. Sipping from his chalice of ambrosia he watched his newest creation bound to and fro.

"I simply adore him!" said Persephone, his queen. "I think I'll name him Cerberus!"

Persephone petted each one of the hound's heads, before throwing three severed arms in rapid succession. The beast raced after them, tearing each asunder with bloody vigour.

"When he grows he will make a fearsome guardian of Tartarus."

www.zoeyxolton.com

The Ice Was So Thin Under the Snow

C. Marry Hultman

Careful not to slip I entered the Castle of Ice. I hoped to find answers, but I was too late. Liquified snow covered the ancient floor, and atop a thawing throne towered great Anguta, his daughter's mutilated body splayed before him.

"You are too late," he intoned, eyes cold. "This world will soon be no more, and I have sent my brothers, sisters and kin to Adlivun. Soon I will follow."

"But why?" I asked.

"Did you not think you had to care for this world?" Anguta hung his head in mourning. "We gave them everything, and you destroyed it."

https://wisconsinnoir.wixsite.com/wi

Twisting Soil
Thomas Wake

Laughter, campfire reflected on the calm waters by an Irish lake. Marshmallows and sausages, hugs and deep kisses.

The forest floor breaks. Happy sounds are replaced by screaming, the creaking of trees and the undulating of the forest floor. Shapes in the shadows of the forest run with fear-granted speed.

A man tumbles over, the soil wrapping around him ferociously and mercilessly as he is eaten alive by the Earth. The woman does not stop, her steps carried by dread and horror.

She releases a lugubrious wail and falls, her eyes rising to see the Horned God.

The hunt begins.

https://twitter.com/ThomasWake12

FERMATA
JESS RHODES

Something stalks Orpheus. Its breath clings, rank and humid, to the nape of his neck. He can't look. To look is to lose her.

But Eurydice doesn't have claws that clack a haunting beat, nor scales that grind against unhewn stone. She doesn't stink of rot and iron.

His stalker moans, the sound rasping against his skull. His Eurydice's voice is a soaring, sweet flute. He imagines fangs ripping into her soft throat. The claws and scales are muffled now, slick with her blood. Louder, closer. Something hot drips onto his neck. A bony talon grasps his shoulder.

Orpheus looks.

Twitter @dead_end_rhodes

THE RITUAL OF AMON
MICHAEL D. NADEAU

The rhythmic beat of the drums would've been soothing, if she weren't tied to a stone slab in the forest. Or anywhere else for that matter, she thought.

Her roommate had invited her to a party, celebrating the moon or something, and as Amy tagged along little did she know that she was the guest of honor.

They were trying to summon someone called Amon, and she couldn't get free. The knife gleamed in the darkness as it rose above her, ready for blood.

Maybe Amon will save me if I ask nicely, she thought.

The darkness answered.

...I might.

BYTTING

TOR-ANDERS ULVEN

In the olden days they were called de underjordiske. Foul creatures living dreadful subterranean lives, envious of the fortuitous humans above. Once in a while they'd crawl to the surface, replacing a human infant with one of their own, offering the dark child a chance at a better life. Bytting, they'd call it. Disturbing, however unbelievable it may be.

Yet I wonder…

Whenever I watch my infant son sleeping I get a creeping suspicion that something isn't right. Maybe it's the look in his eyes, a crooked fingernail, something.

I don't want to hurt him, but can I risk it?

https://www.facebook.com/hyperobscure/
https://www.reddit.com/user/hyperobscura

SHE OF SEVEN NAMES
KATHLEEN HALECKI

The newborn babe lies sleeping, unaware of the danger that lurks in the dark. There is no sound as She of Seven Names, Lamaštu, crawls up from the floor to leer down into the cot with her twisted lion's face and pendulous breasts. The child recoils as blood-stained hands reach out to drag crooked talons over his skin, sinking them deep within his flesh.

The mother wakens and instinctively draws her child closer to her, slipping the bronze amulet of Pazuzu around him and whispering urgent prayers of protection.

The thwarted demon slinks away, searching the night for easier prey.

GUARDIANS OF THE GRAVE
DEREK DUNN

Heavy footsteps beat the untrodden path, sending a cloud of dust into the still air. The graveyard had been undisturbed for centuries—until now. As Jerrick and his men raided the island, bodies shook in the ground below.

The men paused at the stench of decay, forcing some to hurl a mess of mead and fish onto the overgrown tombs. Jerrick pressed forward, ready to unearth the forgotten treasures.

But the Draugr would not relent.

The undead creatures rose from the graves, crushing the intruders with brute strength until only Jerrick remained. The broad-shouldered man would make the perfect feast.

Twitter: @DerekTDunn

GOD OF GODS
CALLUM PEARCE

The God of Gods surveyed his subjects, and they stared back hungrily. For centuries they had circled him, each slithering closer to his throne. All of them dreamed of the day they would strike.

Who would it be that would come for his crown, become the ruler of all? He watched, and waited.

It was the first, and favourite, of his sons that dared. The one god he hadn't been watching.

Bleeding from the throat, attacked from behind, he couldn't help but feel a little pride as he slumped off his throne and his son snatched the crown from his corpse.

Gravestone Anguish
Mark Anthony Smith

You can hear her anguish from the dark, attic window if you pass the cemetery at night. She screams like an animal. I can hear her hooves on the wooden floor. She paces, lashing out at the locked door.

Imelda no longer recognizes me with those demonic eyes. I long to return my wife to her former self, to the lover before I dabbled.

Creep at night, around the cold stones of the dead, and you'll hear something to melt your marrow. Her goatish gait paces until the darkest hour, then she'll break free and I shall conjure no more.

Twitter: @MarkAnthonySm16
Facebook: Mark Anthony Smith- Author

ICARUS AND THE MINOTAUR
NOA COVO

Brothers, raised in the womb of the Labyrinth as living punishments. Deformed sons from genius men that tricked their way to divinity, sentencing their sons to monstrosity.

Daedalus rescues Icarus from the Labyrinth, leaving the Minotaur to die.

With the sun in his face Icarus understands how this must go. He is not better than the bull-headed boy, who died at the hands of a prince.

Icarus will die at no hand but his own.

When he climbs high into the sky the feathers join his skin, and once again his father has created something that will haunt him forever.

Twitter @covo_noa

Demon Mbwiri
Drew Starling

The fetish priest walked into the hut. He gazed at the boy, lying in the dirt. The child's eyes were white, his mouth open, his blood tainted. The boy's mother held him and wept.

"Please, save my son!"

The boy released a scream not from this world, his body suddenly whipping and flipping.

The priest knew this boy had been taken, his soul compromised. The demon Mbwiri had come right in. He reached behind his back and gathered the blade. He cut the child open and watched his life spill out.

"There," said the fetish priest, "I have saved him."

Twitter: @ScaryStarling

THE WRONG NEIGHBORHOOD
KIMBERLY REI

The routine spacewalk from Station Epsilon had gone smoothly. Two engineers, half a dozen repairs, one minor scare. Dropping a tool shouldn't cause distress, and chasing after it was certainly a poor choice, but the engineer was tethered. Once his partner stopped laughing, he was rescued.

Everyone enjoyed a good chuckle when the poor man spoke of an invisible hand swatting the screwdriver out of his grip, so he hid the bruise forming across his fingers. He hid the memory of the voice in his ear, mocking, and he hid the previous team's log of a restless god seeking worshipers.

http://tales.studiorei.org/

Shelter
Elizabeth Nettleton

"You're a troll," she cried.

"You're lost," I replied.

The rain clung to her tunic, heavy against her skin. She glanced behind her, and back at me, unsure. My candle flickered, painting shadows on the cave walls.

Her hands trembled, recalling storybooks and nightmares about my kind. But this storm was fiercer than any dream, so she stepped toward me.

"May I take shelter here?"

I acceded with a smile. Leading her deeper into the mountain, darkness greeted us with a kiss.

Then I curled my knotted hand around her throat.

"Why?" she gasped, clawing at her neck.

"Why not?"

Twitter: @ElizabethNett18
https://elizabeth-nettleton.webnode.com/

LIGHT AS A FEATHER
MELODY GRACE

Light as a feather, stiff as a board.
This was a ritual that was long adored.
Until the night the board would break,
Along with the life of our dear classmate.

We gathered around, hands held out,
Shouting the words as she lay without doubt.
That's when the demon appeared in the dark,
Fingers like knives as he reached for her heart.

She tried to scream, but it was to no avail.
Her heart dropped below the feather on the scale.

The life faded from her eyes as he took her soul.
Light as a feather, stiff as a board.

SQUALLS OF SORROW
N.M. BROWN

Wails of sorrow tormented bayside residents through torrents of rain.

The banshee was mourning, but for whom was yet to be determined. Families held their loved ones tight, staying inside at the slightest hint of gloomy weather.

Finally the long-awaited day came. Townsfolk lingered with bated breath as Mrs. Applebaum shuddered through her last moments. People breathed easy, assuming the banshee's prophecy was fulfilled.

A squall came, catching our town off guard. Some didn't have time to seek shelter, myself included.

From gusts of wind a siren of grief bellows through the clouds, and I think it's meant for me.

POSEIDON'S REVENGE
PATRICIA ELLIOTT

Rhode grabbed the ship's railing, using her other hand to shield her eyes from the heavy rain and wind. Her heart raced within her, tears forming. He found them, as she knew he would.

"Father, stop!"

"Never! Human's must learn that our species don't mix." Poseidon struck the ocean's surface with his trident, sending a giant wave towards the sailors. Soon his daughter would be his again.

She clung to her lover. "I won't go with you, I'd rather die with Alexios."

"Then so be it!"

Raising his hands, he summoned a lightning bolt and split the boat in two.

www.facebook.com/AuthorPatriciaElliott
www.twitter.com/AuthorPatricia

THE MONSTER'S MOON
SHELDON WOODBURY

The eerie myth of the Monster's Moon foretells what will happen when the ghoulish world, that's a shadow of ours, is suddenly unleashed in all its nightmarish glory.

It will be the end of days when macabre creatures and terrifying creations storm out with nothing but a ravenous desire for chaos and carnage. Fire and blood will surge to the sky, the air filled with the clattering of bones.

This brings us to a question you need to consider before the sun sets: How will you feel when you gaze up and see the moon blink with a creepy delight?

http://sheldonwoodbury.blogspot.com/

TARTARUCHI

TIMOTHY FRIESENHAHN

Tartaruchi's voice oozed malevolence, the being taking sadistic pleasure in torturing its victims.

"Scream, you helpless heap of breathing flesh! There is no escape once my hooks penetrate your flesh, so go ahead and beg for mercy."

Tartaruchi ripped and tore at the flesh of all new inhabitants of Hell, as was his duty.

Once dead they would return to life repeatedly, and endure this punishment for all eternity. A coppery scent lingered in the air, nefarious laughs escaping him as his victim's innards hit the floor. He watched as the light faded from their eyes, his job finally done.

www.twitter/@timfriesenhahn
www.facebook.com/timothy.friesenhahn.7

May Queen

Hannah Hulbert

Flora watches the procession from the blossoming hawthorn tangle. Girls in white skip past and Morris dancers jingle and clack, a flurry of ribbons. She tenses, seething with indignation. They perform their ritual, but she has not been invited. Thirteen pretty virgins giggle as they weave threads around the pole on the green, treading patterns into the grass.

Dusk settles, bonfires are lit, and one is crowned Queen. They don't leap through the flames, and they've forgotten why they ever did. Flora slides out of the thicket as the people drift homewards, licking her lips. Tonight she will remind them.

Twitter: @hhulbert

THE CHINVAT BRIDGE
CHARLES REIS

As his body quivered Eshaq stepped on a bridge narrower than his feet. Goosebumps covered his skin as two black, four-eyed dogs snarled behind him. Retreat wasn't possible. Walking foot-over-foot he looked upward at the night sky, ignoring the abyss below.

He stopped and closed his eyes, regret filling his soul over his life of debauchery. Now judgment in the afterlife demanded that he face this difficult walk over the Chinvat Bridge.

When he opened them he gasped. A nude old woman, with blistering skin, floated before him. Laughing, she pushed Eshaq. His screams endured until he entered the void.

www.facebook.com/charles.reis.35
www.instagram.com/cthulhudawn1979/

Winging It

Emma K. Leadley

The crow's wings left a shadow of dark velvet crossing the earth as he flew. The world was more complex to navigate than it used to be, full of metal and glass.

Towers raised skywards, endless numbers of flying machines, light everywhere. He missed the good old days, when you could peck out the eyes of a corpse on the battlefield or navigate by the stars. He wasn't even sure when it was, or who he was, anymore.

Thought...? Memory...? But, he knew where he was going. Every day he flew the globe, arriving home for dinner. Old habits for old familiars.

www.emmaleadley.co.uk
www.twitter.com/autoerraticism

Raising Hell

Yvonne Glasgow

The darkness of the night hid what was happening in the cemetery, though anyone nearby would hear the sounds of chanting.

"Awaken, awaken, awaken!"

The echoes floated gently on the breeze, rustling the leaves. The large moon hung low. It was a super moon, which brought about the perfect night to call forth one of the Old Ones, slumbering beneath the ground.

Three dark figures, shrouded in shadows from a mausoleum, stood wrapped in robes. The ground shuddered below them, then burst open. Flames shot forth, incinerating the chanting trio.

Hades rose from the dirt, ablaze.

"I'm awake!" he growled.

https://www.facebook.com/glassgoatpublishing/
https://www.facebook.com/dreamsanddivination/

NEMESIS

SANDY BUTCHERS

The boat rocked heavily in the foaming waves, and Hymir held on for dear life. When the waves started to foam, and from the froth rose a giant serpent, he knew that Thor had found his match.

Thor grabbed his hammer and struck the horrid creature with all his might, a deep crimson coloring the waves. The serpent hissed and slithered, spitting acid from the fume of corpses that was its breath. Coiling around the boat it crushed the master of the mighty hammer, but Thor refused to surrender. He roared and struck again and again, until the beast collapsed.

http://www.sandybutchers.com
https://www.facebook.com/AuthorSandyButchers/

Amarok

Chris Bannor

They forgot his name, these lesser creatures who fled instead of fighting. It was unforgivable! These same people used to quiver when the ground shook under his paws.

Their villages had changed, as had their weapons, but none were as mighty as Amarok. He left a stinking, bloody trail behind him, waiting to see if any were brave enough to follow and face him.

He was Amarok, the mightiest of the giant wolves. He was not afraid of their warriors, or their steel. He challenged them with every breath, and he would make them bleed until his name was remembered.

Facebook: @chrisbannorauthor
www.ChrisBannor.com

Naughty or Nice?

Nerisha Kemraj

"What do you mean no naughty children, Nicholas? There's always miscreants! Give me the list!"

"No, Krampus! Not this again. You'll never get your hands on this. Naughty children get no gifts. That's their punishment, not you!"

Santa slammed the door on a sullen Krampus. His horns burned red with fury. No matter, he'll grab those naughty kids on Krampusnacht. List or not, nothing could stop him.

His green eyes blazed as he descended upon a small town. Soon he was dragging his rucksack of screaming children into his waiting lair.

"Time to learn how to be nice," he cackled.

https://www.amazon.com/author/nerisha_kemraj
https://www.facebook.com/pg/Nerishakemrajwriter/
https://www.instagram.com/nerishakemraj

Hera's Revenge

Amber M. Simpson

Lamia's screams echo off the dense cave walls as she lies naked, moaning in pain. When the baby slides out in a gush of blood, she whimpers in relief.

Hera steps from the shadows and Lamia gasps, clutching the baby to her chest.

"Please," she sobs, cringing away. "This one does not belong to Zeus."

But the goddess cares not. "Eat."

Lamia shrieks in protest, but cannot stop from devouring the infant from head to toe, punishment for Zeus' love.

"Well done," says Hera. Lamia howls in anguish at the loss of yet another child from the goddess' vengeful cruelty.

https://ambermsimpson.com/
https://www.facebook.com/authorambermsimpson/

A Pact Fulfilled

Jen Chichester

"Time to pay up." He extended a chubby hand. "The deed is done. Fulfill the pact."

Nyam unsheathed the dagger that had spilled blood under his family name for centuries. He handed it hilt-forward to the bakru, who took it with a thievish glint in his ruby eyes.

"It has caused enough trouble. All I ask is that you leave my people and our woods in peace."

The bakru tsked, waving a fat little finger in front of his face. "Soon you will see ghost-white faces smeared in your people's blood. Look for their ships to settle on your shores."

www.facebook.com/JenChichesterWritesStuff/
Instagram: @hopelesspierrot

Huitzilopochtli's Heart
K.B. Elijah

The sun was at its zenith, that mystical time when no shadows lingered in the world, the glow of the sun god spreading good fortune.

The man lay on top of the temple, as close as he could be to the sky, and a smile danced on his lips.

That smile caved to agony as the Aztec priest carved open his abdomen and held his still-beating heart to the sky.

"Istli," he whispered. "Take this offering, Great One, this fragment of sun, and continue to bless us with your radiance."

The god laughed cruelly, and plunged the world into darkness.

Twitter: @KBElijah1
Instagram: @k.b.elijah

Carnivore of Crete

N.M. Brown

Our area of Greece experiences tragedy every seven years. The vengeful choices of Minos still ripple into our lives. A creature created out of hate and jealousy needs to be satiated.

Every cycle the beast comes, taking children to its maze of death. Killing, then eating. The town rages, mourns, and forgets, until the cycle renews for those lucky enough to still be alive to see it.

Or unlucky, if you're a parent.

The year of the cycle has come around again, and I'm determined to protect our children. My name is Theseus, and today I will slaughter the Minotaur.

WILL-O-WISPS

PAUL BENKENDORFER

Nights like this are when the bog is most dangerous; when the Ignis Fatuus, the Will-o-wisps, hunt. They disguise themselves as candlelights to lure travelers into the bog, then drown them.

The fog is blinding. Only a lantern illuminates and warms our path along the cold, dark road as two flickering lights appear before us. My companion points, and suggests that we follow them.

I tell him not to go.

He does not listen, vanishing into the mist. There is a scream, followed by a splash. The flickering lights strike like vultures, going dark seconds later.

The bog goes silent.

https://twitter.com/PBenkendorfer

ECHOED EXPERIENCE
KERRY E.B. BLACK

In the glade a golden man savors the splendor of my mountain. His profile belies aristocracy, his designer hiking clothes reeking of privilege.

I can't speak, and haven't since the curse. Damn Hera for punishing me for her husband's indiscretions!

The hiker touches an aspen trunk, broader than his body. His lips part, an enraptured gasp. The narcissist is unaware of anything, or anyone, but himself.

So like Aphrodite's disciple. I bet this one loves his reflection too.

I charge, a vengeful wind, as I have so many times.

His beauty shatters upon the rocks, I echo his dying breath.

https://www.goodreads.com/author/show/
7874880.Kerry_E_B_Black
https://twitter.com/BlackKerryblick

THE UNWANTED VISITOR
SANDY BUTCHERS

The sweet scent of mead had seeped into every crack and corner of the hall, as they knew that it would lure the beast like a bee towards honey. It was quiet, so deadly quiet, as the men sat waiting with their swords and daggers drawn.

The floorboards of the front porch creaked, and the door groaned when it opened slightly. Quickly the smell of the sweet, honeyed wine gave way to the horrid stench of putrefaction. Blood shimmered in the candlelight when a decapitated head was thrown into the hall.

"It's him," one of the men whispered, "It's Grendel…"

http://www.sandybutchers.com
https://www.facebook.com/AuthorSandyButchers/

Water Witch
Grant Hinton

I smell steel's bite, the hot metallic blood and the dank lichen on the cave walls. A dragon and a monster lay dead, but the mother is still here.

I creep forward. My people will not rest until she is slain. My body is shocked, arm muscles bunch as I raise my sword, a wicked shriek splitting the damp air. A hand moves over by the wall.

Lichen, moss and seaweed cling to the undulating surface. Grendel's mother peels off the wall. If I fail, she will kill them all. I smell the blood again, and remember that's it's mine.

THE SUMMONING

JOEL R. HUNT

The Voice had been given many names throughout the millennia: *'Ahriman'*. *'Erlik'*. *'Iblis'*.

This creature had used 'Lucifer'.

"Master," the human was saying, "we are ready to begin the summoning. What do you need of us?"

Three humans for sacrifice, intoned the Voice. The human's soul flickered with uncertainty.

"Is that all, master? The ancient tomes tell of seventeen sacrifices."

You dare question me?

The human's soul flinched.

"Never, Master Lucifer. We shall bring you the sacrifices you require."

The human was correct, in a way. It did require seventeen souls for the ritual, but fortunately there were fourteen cultists.

https://twitter.com/JoelRHunt1
https://www.reddit.com/r/JRHEvilInc/

La Cegua

Sarah Matthews

Santiago followed the raven-haired woman into the murky alleyway, intoxicated by the smell of her perfume and by the copious amount of beer he had consumed.

They intertwined, her lips nuzzling against his ear, her warm breath sending a shiver of pleasure down his spine. Beneath her perfume Santiago noticed the strong scent of horses, but he ignored it and pressed closer against her.

She bit his ear hard, his head snapping back. An equine skull grinned at him where once had been a beautiful woman's face.

It leaned in, whispers of madness falling from its bone lips.

Santiago screamed.

Twitter @superbfinch

REUNITED
Ryan Rosenberry

When I first beheld the beast, for it could be nothing less, my loathing peaked and I could not step away.

The beast held in its claw the object of my quest. Retrieving said object seemed pointless, for his body held no life and hung together in bits and fragments. Yet my queen demanded this of me, fetching her secret while the King protects the land.

I decided to lure the beast back to her, the veil queen. What pleasure it will be to reunite her with her lover, smeared together in the claws of the monstrosity. Two becomes one.

METASTATIC
JESS RHODES

Spring. Persephone emerges, gaunt with winter shadows. She coaxes crops to sprout, fingers wriggling beneath the dirt. But the sunless waters of the Acheron seep from beneath her nails. The grain is black with ergot.

The women pray. She eases babies into mothers' wombs. Her hands slip. Growths blossom, riotous and vicious. They have the frozen teeth of her husband's domain and the overripe gluttony of her mother's harvest. They smother from the inside.

Her husband's hands are scars under her skin, her mother's embrace a noose around her neck. Persephone is the goddess of new life, and she rots.

Twitter @dead_end_rhodes.

Arrondi's Last Stand
Jim Bates

Arrondi stood frozen as the Basilisk made its way toward him, a giant, snake-like creature slithering through the jungle. It licked its fangs, saliva dripping.

Why couldn't he move? It must be the legendary spell.

Uncontrollable fear caused him to retch as the Basilisk began wrapping its body around him. He pounded the thick, slimy skin with his fists, but the monster was determined. Tighter and tighter it squeezed, until Arrondi began losing consciousness.

He released one final scream as the air was forced from his lungs, the sound of ribs cracking and blood gushing the last thing he heard.

www.theviewfromlonglake.wordpress.com

Destined

Heidi Ann Willits

The fire licked at my skin as my sisters and I spun around, each of us draped in white. Ethereal swirls of gossamer acted as both a physical and magical veil between two realities.

As I bounded in and out of our world I felt the darkness creep in. I looked to my family, but they were dancing, chanting, twirling in a circle light as air, but I felt drawn to the ground.

When I could dance no longer I crashed to my resting place. They didn't stop dancing. I became one with the earth.

Sacrificial.

This was my purpose.

https://twitter.com/heidiwillits
https://www.facebook.com/Heidi-Ann-Willits-100217031460654/

Sealed Away

Michael D. Nadeau

She pressed the block, activating the door, and dust fell down around her. This tomb was older than anything they had found yet, and the dry Egyptian heat couldn't touch her this deep.

The dark room beckoned her, its silence taunting her. She crept in and brushed the dust away from the plaque on the far wall. The ancient hieroglyphics naming the mystery man buried here as foreign. Through another arch she saw the sarcophagus, no likeness carved in bas relief.

The name etched on the lid was simple, written in Aramaic, and it shocked her to her core: Cain.

RESURRECTION
NERISHA KEMRAJ

Marie uttered the last line of the spell, drizzling her blood onto the five-pointed star. Candle wax dripped onto Jason's jacket, lying in the pentagram's center.

A sudden flash of light blinded her as the flame extinguished.

Adjusting to darkness Marie exhaled, elated as a figure emerged from the star's core.

It worked! The Lord of Death had returned Jason to her!

"There'll be an exchange of souls to complete the ritual," the Priestess had told her.

She was wrong, I'm still alive.

It was only when she looked inside the crib that Marie realised her baby breathed no more.

https://www.amazon.com/author/nerisha_kemraj
https://www.facebook.com/pg/Nerishakemrajwriter/
https://www.instagram.com/nerishakemraj

BEWARE THE KELPIE

DAVID A.F. BROWN

The boys spot the stallion by the water. "Touch it!" they dare.

Angus approaches the horse. Making gentle contact he traces his fingers over its coarse, black mane, commanding the beast with a steadfast glare.

He mounts its back. His friends cheer in awe, until a shrill scream erupts. "My hand is stuck!"

Angus tugs hard, but the mane snakes around his body, gripping limbs and snapping bones. As the horse returns to the deep loch, Angus' howls turn into gurgles.

Mouths agape, the boys watch helplessly as their friend's entrails surge to the surface in a burst of crimson.

www.facebook.com/browndavidaf

THE BOGGART
RUSSELL SMEATON

My new house was old, nestled against an ancient forest. Naked footprints, with oh-so-long toes, soon began to appear.

The creature enjoyed stealing my morning milk delivery.

Leaving a saucer of milk one night solved the problem: no more theft, and even a tidy yard. Locals warned me, but I didn't listen.

When I forgot to leave milk one night things descended into madness. The yard was trashed, broken glass everywhere.

I've escaped back in the city, where there's safety in numbers.

This morning my car mirrors were broken, the saucer of milk untouched. I'm seriously considering leaving the country.

https://www.facebook.com/tikirussy/
www.amazon.co.uk/Russell-Smeaton/e/B06XSYJ8TP

Touchdown
DeBickel

The students had crouched beneath desks and tables as thunderous winds ripped the school roof off. Everyone survived the tornado, though Kenny was spouting nonsense.

"I saw monsters! They took the roof!"

His English teacher, Mr. Diaz, thought Kenny was just high again.

The students picked up things as they left, though soon a student screamed. Mr. Diaz came running as a girl pointed at a creature laying in a trashed hallway. The lower half was clearly avian, with sharp talons and wings, but the upper half …

"Mr. Diaz, that's what Kenny saw!"

Mr. Diaz choked. "A harpy?"

SOMETHING IN THE SOIL
ARNIE MAY

Their greed had poisoned them.

It had led to their unquenchable want, to their revolt, and, as far as they'd believed, his death. The same soil he had fertilized and tilled they made his grave.

His unfathomably-deep sedation wore off, giving way to vengeance. He felt their presence above. Surely they were just as ungrateful, always forgetting last year's fruitful harvest in one thought of the next.

He disturbed the hundred-year-old earth encasing his mighty limbs. Roots snapped and trees sank. How foolish of them to forget such rough treatment, he thought. He wouldn't be quick to do the same.

Twitter: @arnie_may

Among the Foxgloves
Elizabeth Nettleton

"You deserve this."

I ran my finger over the blade of my dagger. She watched me, her face pale and her mouth open, spittle dripping through her teeth and onto her chin. Her hand grabbed at the air, but the stars wouldn't save her. No, not tonight. They saw what she did to me.

"You destroyed my home."

Her legs thrashed above me, kicking feebly. I flicked my wrist and she fell, a blanket of green faerie dust falling with her. My wings opened, and I pressed my dagger against her throat.

"Do you feel like picking my flowers now?"

Twitter: @ElizabethNett18
https://elizabeth-nettleton.webnode.com/

THE DEMON STAR
ANN WYCOFF

True magic is hatched by innocent pain, hence the Sorcerer coveted suffering without end for his carnivorous spells.

Revulsion.

Ruination.

Rebirth.

Diviners of songs exposed his moment of supreme vulnerability. Warriors seized, then bound him to a stake upon the blessed pyre.

"Kindle the sacred flame! Dance!"

A star in Gazelle's horn burst into a coruscating blaze of bloody light, as if waiting trillions of lifetimes for this moment, and the Alkebulan night wore a hungry demon's face.

A hideous strength.

The mob fled as one.

Uncleanliness oozed out from distant fever trees, loosening the Sorcerer's bonds.

Vindication.

Victory.

Vengeance.

www.annwycoff.com

THE SPRUCE BOG
BRYAN DYKE

The war-party halts for a moment, frozen in time, their faces shifting from focused to terrified. I try to speak, but what comes out is a noise like scraping tree boughs. The spruce clamors, and the bog revolts in my wake.

The warriors drop their tomahawks and run.

"Wen-di-go!" one screams.

Wendigo?

The name means nothing to me as they flee.

I look down to the bog and observe my reflection. A tawny body, bleached skin, clumped fur, and eyes that glow blood-red.

I do not care. I am no longer cold and tired; instead I hunger for human flesh.

AN END TO SUFFERING

MATTHEW A. CLARKE

The battle rages around me, indifferent to my suffering. I writhe in blood-slicked ash, clutching at my mangled face.

Bristled hairs, warm and tacky, seep through my fingers, sliding from flesh that is no more than lumpy paste.

Bjorn lands hard beside me, his legs lashed to ribbons. A barbed arrow tip glints red through the back of his skull.

I grasp his calloused hand in one of mine, feeling my face collapse as I look up at the dark, burning heavens.

Valkyries breach the thundering clouds, and my vision begins to wane.

I whisper, "See you in Valhalla, brother."

Gryla's Tradition
Brian Rosenberger

She hears the bells, the songs from the village, but pays little notice. She's more intent on the purrs from Jólaköttur, her black cat, keeping one ear cocked to the insults exchanged between her lads as they hurl rotten potatoes at each other.

They grow restless.

She's restless too as she stirs the pot. Soon it will be time to leave the cave, to lumber south. The bells continue to chime. She listens for voices of naughty children, music to her oversized ears. The voices draw closer. Gryla sips, tasting. The key ingredient was still missing, but not for long.

ENTRY TO VALHALLA
KASE GLIDEWELL

Thunder rumbled, a hammer struck.

A murder of crows lifted off the ground and took to the air. The blood had caked and dried on Odin's face, as black as the feathers of his crows.

Einar stood over the broken bodies of his fallen friends, their dead eyes staring to the heavens. He shakily picked up his axe.

"I won't join you today." Einar said.

Odin shook his head. "Your friends already have."

Einar wiped the blood from his face and hefted his shield up. This would be it. With a cry, he rushed towards Odin's spear, ready to die.

https://twitter.com/kaseman742
https://www.instagram.com/kaseman742/

Andromeda's Fate
Faith Pierce

They bind me, strip me.

She orders it, but my hair she does herself. Grasping handfuls, shearing it away, tossing it into the ocean that crashes at my bare feet against the rocks.

Every day since the first I can remember, she has held my hair in her hands and told me I am beautiful. That day, I learned it was with envy.

They rip me apart. One trillion pieces, offered to the sky.

Later she tells the story of her enemies taking me, a tale of a daring rescue by a half-god.

I watch, trapped in my starry prison.

Twitter @faithepierce

FREE CANDY
GABRIELLA BALCOM

Opening the door of her hut Baba Yaga stepped outside, waving a hand at her home.

Ten-year-old Andi skipped along hours later. She gasped at the cookie-shaped house covered in treats, and the "Free Candy" sign.

Sweets were everywhere inside, and she stuffed handfuls into her mouth.

Baba Yaga appeared before her, ripping off the girl's right arm and sucking the bloody end before devouring it.

Andi collapsed, screaming hysterically.

Using a long, jagged fingernail the witch beheaded her, cackling as blood spurted out. Baba Yaga gnawed straight through the child's skull and into the brain, eagerly smacking her lips.

https://m.facebook.com/GabriellaBalcom.lonestarauthor

FRIENDSHIP REPAID

ANN WYCOFF

For years, my "friend" boasted of his good fortune, and sneered at my poverty.

Then....

"Will you sponsor my nephew Petre for the Mystery?"

I was an initiate, who knew a deep secret.

"Drink!"

Petre drank.

"Nepenthe," we chanted.

We lowered him into a waiting *pithos*.

"Descend into darkness."

Virgins tossed pomegranate seeds and amaranth into the jar over him.

Horns brayed.

Initiates sealed the vessel with a leaden stopper.

Suffocate, Petre, inside your coffin jar!

The secret?

Thousands lie fermenting beneath the temple. Only masters may feast upon the delicacies contained within the *pithoi*.

www.annwycoff.com

ORIGIN
HOLLEY CORNETTO

The stones stood in a perfect circle. There were no fires, yet the evening breeze carried with it the scent of burning leaves. Within the sleeping earth something stirred. A bolt of lightning cracked across the sky, splitting the largest stone to its core. The chanting grew louder, cries of man and creature alike mingled in the darkness. Wine was poured over the severed stone, and into the broken earth.

What once was valley is now a swelled, pregnant belly of rolling hills. Gaia will soon give birth. Oh, Mother of Titans, what monsters shall you deliver forth this time?

Twitter @HLCornetto

CHOSEN
K.T. TATE

The gate opens! Outer gods, maddening and obscene, pull themselves into our reality. Chaos reigns as the sky turns unspeakable. Standing steadfast we admire its beauty.

I was just a child when I made a pact. Bloody and broken I'd cried out; that's when the void answered. Their messenger, a pitch nightmare, still less terrifying than my abusers.

I became their key. I learned their rites, leaving ancient symbols graffitied across the world. Secret places became contaminated with their lore, the stars aligned and the world lit up. Now I stand with their obsidian envoy, watching the world burn.

https://eldritch-hollow.com/

THE DULLAHAN
DREW STARLING

O’er borough and bog rides the death dealing Dullahan.
Through Kilmaine and Cork, through Galway and Tullaghan.
On a brindle-black mare clad in steel-plated mail,
Headless devourer spreading fear through the vale.
Ivory white skull grinning in elbow’s crook,
Freezes Dullahan’s prey with no more than a look.
Whip made of bone, of the spine from its victims,
Lashes folly-found men who believe they have tricked him.
Dullahan, Dullahan ride far away from this place!
Let innocent men die with honor and grace.
Dullahan, Dullahan we’ll give thee a crown,
If you spare us tonight, and strike the next town.

Twitter @ScaryStarling

BINDING AGREEMENT
KIM PLASKET

"**N**ever open an email entitled Binding Agreement, unless you want to suffer."

Those words came back to me as I read the email. Text of the email said, "In ancient times the curse was read. I bind you to death meaning the one who reads will die."

I felt my skin boiling, blood leaking from my ears as the curse began to take effect. I knew one day I'd die, but didn't think it would be so soon. My life was over, but I had misery to spread.

I entered several names, and my last action was to press 'Forward'.

https://www.amazon.com/-/e/B074YCLRCF

BLOOD IN SAND
ALICE DE SAMPAIO

"There's a difference between lonely and lonesome. The latter is by choice, and filled with content. Believe me, I know."

The soldier next to him shivered in fear, but Polemos didn't care. He was here to fight, not to comfort the meek.

His sword longed for blood. With every strike Polemos felt more like himself. Blood looked pretty on sand, and it never looked prettier than in the sands of Troy. Polemos charged, his war cry spearing through his opponents' bones.

He was battle.

He was despair.

He was war.

The bodies piling at his feet were a worthy sacrifice.

www.ravensandbooks.tumblr.com

https://alicedesampaio.blogspot.com/p/readers-list.html

THE BLOOD

CHRIS BANNOR

The rain fell heavy around him. Not even the thick canopy of trees could stop the water as it fell over broad shoulders covered in ritualistic glyphs. Blood dripped from his curved blade, falling into muddied footprints as he continued on his quest.

There was nowhere they could hide. He was the ancient god of a long-forgotten people, but their blood still called to him. As the slaughter continued he heard their pleas. They would remember him once more. Outsiders would remember to fear him, and his people would love him.

Then the Blood would rise once more.

Facebook: @chrisbannorauthor
www.ChrisBannor.com

THE WATER
CALLUM PEARCE

The water goddess had returned to take us all.

The ice was melting, the seas rising. She desired me today. She whispers behind the rain, speaking to me through running taps.

"Come home."

At the beach I lowered myself into the sand. I felt it shift and slide, moulding around me. I waited patiently for the hungry waves to claim me. She would come for everyone, but momentarily she spoke only to me.

The waves whispered welcomes and crept closer, swallowing me up. The stench of filth crept up my nostrils and coated my tongue, followed by dirty, dark saltwater.

https://mobile.twitter.com/Aladdinsane79
https://m.facebook.com/calmpeace13/

UNDER THE CHAPEL

JOEL R. HUNT

"Come in, come in. You must be exhausted!"

The stranger stomped snow from his boots and perched on the end of a pew. Father Dullaney brought over a candle to warm his hands.

"We don't often get travellers to the chapel at this time of night. There are dangerous creatures in these woods, you know."

"And demons buried underground, I hear," grumbled the stranger.

"True," said Father Dullaney, "but fear not. Whilever this chapel houses a priest of true faith, no demon shall wake from their slumber."

"Aye, heard that too."

A knife glinted through candlelight, and demons awoke below.

https://twitter.com/JoelRHunt1
https://www.reddit.com/r/JRHEvilInc/

God of Water

Charlotte O'Farrell

I was one of the most important gods in the pantheon. My statue stood prominently in the temple, adorned with gems.

Oh, I was generous to my people! I was God of Water, keeping drought and floods alike at bay. Then irrigation came; science made me obsolete. Water held no fear for them now.

Over decades I lost followers. No offerings came. My statue was moved to a tiny chapel, gathering dust.

This year the entire city will be swept away by monstrous storms. They will pay for their fickleness! I was God of Water, now I'm God of Vengeance.

Twitter: @ChaOFarrell
Facebook: @AuthorCharlotteOFarrell

NOT TO BE UNDERESTIMATED
GALINA TREFIL

None of the recently-slain, assembled souls before her had ever seen a cat before. All had assumed that felines must be huge, ferocious beasts, with muscles like tree stumps. Otherwise, how could they ever pull the Goddess' chariot?

"Not with might, but magic," Freyja clarified, lifting up and cradling one of the long-haired, big-eyed creatures.

One small-boned, axe-wielding shield maiden, still covered in wet, slick blood from her final battle, reached out to stroke the creature's fur.

She too knew what it was to be underestimated, and diminutive size would stop neither of them from dining with the great warriors.

https://www.facebook.com/Rabbi-Galina-Trefil-535886443115467/

https://galinatrefil.wordpress.com/

THE MYLING
GRANT HINTON

Freya's day was fraught with grief. A murdered child at breakfast, then a car accident at lunch.

Fourteen hours flat on her feet, but the walk home through the Scandinavian cold was nice, if not a little tiring.

With every step she felt more drained, more empty.

"Just a little further," a voice said in her head.

She obeyed.

Freya didn't question the increasing weight on her back nor her path when it veered to the cemetery. Too tired and weighed down was she.

"Nearly there," said the ghostly outline of a child on her back. "Nearly there."

She obeyed.

THE REBIRTHING PROCESS
RON DAVIS

He held his hand, blood dripping from the insignia carved into his palm, over the pregnant woman's immensely swollen midsection. She struggled, crying, against the ropes that bound her to the bed frame with what little strength she had left. The old man picked up a tattered, ancient looking tome of incantations. As he read the single candle lighting the room began to flicker, and the woman's screams intensified. He touched the candle to the fabric of his robe.

"Now is the time, this is the hour. With these words, I will be reborn and I shall be called Phoenix."

https://www.facebook.com/RonDavisAuthor
Twitter @RonDavis1980.

THE MAN-KILLER
BRYAN DYKE

I raise my knife as snow pelts me through the pines.

The tiger roars, its jade eyes pool-like and its mouth frothing.

Kali.

I see her within its pupils. She is a reaper, and I a man afraid. Her myriad arms fan within the cat's eyes, talwars in each hand. She has killed untold men, and there will be a mountain more piled under her paws. Through space, and time, the bloodlust of this goddess will not end.

Kali.

I awake in my bed, an old man in a cold sweat, and realize she comes for me even in dreams.

The Hand of Glory
Willem V. Much

Marya loved her father. She held his left hand by the exposed ulna, the words he gave her pouring out into the cold night air. The hand's fingers twitched, seeking the burning candle she held in her right hand. She imagined a door of bone and iron, just as he taught her. She did not make a sound when it appeared.

Her father called death a thief, and spoke of justice often. A dead thief's hand could open a locked door. Marya imagined the countless souls her father stole from the Underworld and smiled.

What could death's own hand open?

https://twitter.com/VeryScholar

DARKNESS DESCENDS
K. R. NOX

I am Apophis. Elder God, Lord of Chaos, The Snake and Encircler of the World. I lie in wait, as I do each day, and as Ra's powers are all but spent—I chase him from the sky in my colossal, monstrous, serpentine form.

Our battle has endured for ages beyond memory, but this time it will be different. Tonight, as darkness descends…it will be forever.

I have starved myself—awaiting the feast.

When I rise from beneath the mantle of the world, I will devour the sun god once and for all. There will be no dawn for mankind.

www.krnox.com

THE FOOL
MATTHEW A CLARKE

Creeping low through towering pines, dull moonlight illuminates our path.

My troops have deserted me at the first sight of danger, as though they'd have something to live for if we don't claim this victory.

A towering shadow in the distance ahead; I freeze and drop to one knee.

The blood of Heracles, staining my blade, drips sporadically onto golden leaves between my sandals.

The God advances. Does it smell my fear?

Blinding light tears through the ancient trees as lighting is hurled in my direction.

It is I that am foolish, not my men. This war cannot be won.

Hunter's Folly

Joshua Borgmann

Blood flowed into the circle. It called to Cernunnos, the Horned One. He woke from long slumber, his antlers rising into the moonlight and his nose inhaling a poisoned world.

He knew not how long he had been absent, but he saw the bodies of the slaughtered deer immediately.

Man had long hunted the beasts of the woods for food and clothing, but these innocents were left to die uselessly. The ancient god walked from the circle, spotting the cottage of the hunters.

He called upon all woodland creatures to show them no mercy.

The age of man was ending.

Bray Road

Jen Chichester

Sheriff Brady wanted to clock out for the night, but the call from a frenzied traveler took him to Bray Road. Brady thought the man was probably drunk or high, since there was no such thing as a wolf-man.

He pulled over where the field met the woods, climbing out of the squad car. Brady took a few steps and shone his flashlight through the dark, dense fog.

He snorted. "Definitely high."

As Brady turned to get back in his car he felt the stabbing pain of massive claws penetrating his pleather jacket. The wolfman pulled Bray into the fog.

www.facebook.com/JenChichesterWritesStuff/
Instagram: @hopelesspierrot

THE SERPENT WHO BURNS
ROBIN BRAID

We awoke to the serpent's roar as it wound its way down the mountain. "Run to the safe place," said Mother, and I dared not look back as David and I clambered over rocks illuminated by the approaching inferno.

The Elders had told stories of the serpent who burns, and a mere tale it had been until that night.

From our nook by the stream we watched that awful glow descending, devouring. Voices echoed, pained and frightened. I held David's hand tight, his eyes glistened in the darkness. We lowered our heads and prayed for everything we knew and loved.

THE FINAL BATTLE
ALANNA ROBERTSON-WEBB

B astet lounged on her jewel-encrusted throne, her tail twitching excitedly by the armrest as she surveyed the crowd below.

They were waiting for bloodshed, as was she.

The goddess was growing restless, and the crowd's anxiety was making her ears twitch. Finally a roar escaped her, her long fangs glinting red in the dying sun as her challenge clamored to the sky above.

This was her final battle with Apep, the evil snake monster, and either she would win or the world would fall into darkness. All humans would die, and the land would suffer.

She couldn't let that happen.

https://arwauthor.wixsite.com/arwauthor
https://www.amazon.com/Alanna-Robertson-Webb/e/
B07LFYJYS5%3Fref=dbs_a_mng_rwt_scns_share

Becoming Me
Alex Steslow

I remember that, as a small child, I used to be afraid of the monsters under my bed and in my closet. The darkness that hung in the corner of my room terrified me to the core.

Then, one day, the Darkness spoke to me. It spoke of a world I would command and bend to my will, needing to only walk into the shadows and embrace the darkness within me.

Now I sit on my throne of shadows, weaving the fates of those who work in the dark. I became the monster I once feared, so very long ago.

CARRION

STACEY JAINE MCINTOSH

They thought of the Gods as almighty beings. No one expected the girl, frail and skinny as she was, to rise up, bear arms and fight back.

No one knew her name, but plenty wanted to. Ravens circled overhead, cawing relentlessly. Only when she appeared in the middle of the open field did they stop. Raising her arms, as if to embrace the world, she cried out.

"I am Cathubodua. My pets and I are hungry!"

"Carrion are not pets," said a villager.

Cathubodua cocked her head to one side, grinning. "You may feast on his eyes first, my pretties."

www.staceyjainemcintosh.com

Praise Ba'al

Charles Reis

Roger awoke to find himself tied to a tree in the middle of a dark forest. His heart pounded against his chest upon seeing his son standing before him while holding a dagger. A bonfire raged several feet away.

"The son you disowned long ago has returned," he said, pressing the cold weapon against his father's cheek. "But he found himself a God who doesn't reject him."

Roger's eyes opened wide when a tall man, with a long face and crowned with a cylindrical headdress, rose from the fire.

"Praise Ba'al!" His son smiled as he slashed his father's throat.

https://www.facebook.com/charles.reis.35
https://www.instagram.com/cthulhudawn1979/

CAZADOR

BRYAN DYKE

Do not utter Her name in the dark of the night. Do not go to that valley to seek Her shrine. Do not remember what is best forgotten, for those who worshipped Her are dead for good reason. Even they, those who recalled that vile cult, have dwindled. Nothing is left of that goddess, save that abominable temple and a lone idol shaped vaguely like a spider.

I have been there, long ago, and upon the base of that effigy was the name Cazador written in smeared, fresh blood.

I tell you again, go not to that place.

LOVE THE SINNER
KIMBERLY REI

They had forgotten, these villagers turned city-dwellers. Once she was revered, but years melted into centuries and they had forgotten her.

And so she waited, watching them drown their grief in chaos and booze. From the shadows, where they refused to look, she drifted a little closer and sipped at their tears. This new era may have sent her into hiding, but she had never completely gone away.

The time was coming, so deliciously soon, when they would need her. Their world was spiraling into disaster and pain, but the Sin Eater would save them.

She would consume them all.

http://tales.studiorei.org/

GÖTTERDÄMMERUNG
PADDY ARMSTRONG

The day started like most days do, though no one knew what to make of it. Meteorologists were at a loss, as an increase in storms and extreme climates went against everything they'd predicted.

Biologists were puzzled by how such a large creature could have stayed hidden in the ocean so long, or why attacks by wildlife saw an increase.

Things only got worse.

Cities caught fire, oceans froze. Wars broke out and brother killed brother, never knowing why. Forsaking science we found answers in myth, but it was too late.

The ship of dead men's nails came into port.

BURNT OFFERINGS

MARK ANTHONY SMITH

The meal tasted bad the first time. I tasted the burnt pork again as I gripped the wicker cage. I should not have come here, to a village with no signposts. No wonder no one knew the way, or its ways.

I know my fate as I appeal to my only God.

The heathens chant for their panopoly. My clothes are singed from flames, the acrid smoke pricking my nostrils. I am to be offered, like their missing children. I implore them to rise above their base intellects, but they know better.

I will burn for their ripe, fruitful harvest.

Twitter: @MarkAnthonySm16
Facebook: Mark Anthony Smith- Author

Not Tonight

Kimberly Rei

Wind blew across the rooftop, fetid and angry. It carried with it a promise of nightmares. At the edge of both structure and air a misshapen creature watched the city writhe. People hurried this way and that, none bothering to look up.

Ichor dripped from ragged talons and splashed, the tiniest of droplets, onto the pavement far below. A minor sound, but enough to cause a babe in a stroller to howl in fear. The canine at her side tilted his head upward.

His expression was clear, "Not tonight, beast. Not ever."

The shadowed creature nodded back, "We shall see."

THOSE WHO SLUMBER

CHRIS BANNOR

Moss covered the stones, and it took hours to carefully uncover the surface to see what lay beneath. The ruins had been lost to time, forgotten by everyone because the tribe of men who walked this path in the rainforest had died away.

When the men began to go missing we thought they'd been scared off by superstition.

We should have paid attention, we should have learned to read the warnings. These people didn't die of natural causes, they were killed by their own god. They had sacrificed themselves to force it into slumber.

We should have let it sleep.

Facebook @chrisbannorauthor
www.ChrisBannor.com

A Memory of Gods
L.P. Hernandez

He wakes with dust in his mouth, surrounded by crumbling idols crafted by long-dead hands. The cave is empty, his altar a ruin.

Where are my children? He gazes at the weathered paintings on the walls, their colors so vibrant in his memory.

No one has spoken his name in a thousand years, and his sadness hardens into something else.

He calls Brother Beetle, and whispers in its ear.

Tell the others to burrow into the cold earth, to find the yellowed bones of my children. Their time of rest is over. I have returned, and I will be worshipped.

www.lphernandez.com

THE WARNING
CALLUM PEARCE

You can still hear it, can't you? I imagine you thought that you could hide from it. Surrounded by your groaning, grinding machines, flickering screens and shivering speakers.

So many distractions and diversions trying desperately to drown out that constant sound at the edge of hearing, that ticking clock that moves frustratingly slowly.

That warning we sent, our message that remains when all other sounds cease.

TICK.

The old Gods are returning.

TOCK.

They are displeased.

Hear that? The multitudes screaming, the roaring of the ground cracking as buildings fall, drowns out all other sounds.

They rise, so start praying

https://mobile.twitter.com/Aladdinsane79
https://m.facebook.com/calmpeace13/

AUTHOR BIOS
FEATURED ALPHABETICALLY BY FIRST NAME

ABIRAN RAVEENTHIRAN is a first-generation born Canadian as many are in the cultural melting pot that is Toronto, Ontario. He has one foot in the culture of his past and one foot in the present culture with views into both. His works are written in a way to merge concepts of the eastern and western culture together; a product mirroring his own identity. In early to mid-2020, Abiran also has upcoming short stories to be published in anthologies by Black Hare Press, CelticFrog Publishing, The Great Void & Soteira Press.

https://www.instagram.com/lightweaversreads/
https://twitter.com/AbiranRavi

AL PROVANCE: I'm a high school teacher and overall geek living in southern New Hampshire with my wife and two kids. I'm drawn to fantasy and science fiction mostly, though horror has a special place in my heart as I grew up reading ghost stories all the way over to Lovecraftian tales.

https://www.facebook.com/Al-Provance
https://twitter.com/somrael

AL-HAZARD is a young independent horror author. His love story with the genre goes back to his days lurking the basement of the only bookshop in town providing books in his native language. While there, he came across the likes of Algernon Blackwood, Gustavo Adolfo Bécquer or Carlos Ruiz Zafón. This inspired him to get involved with the horror fiction community. To the date, this has successfully landed his work in anthologies such as Horror d'oeuvres (volumes II and III), the Monstronomicon and Scary Snippet's Christmas special.

ALANNA ROBERTSON-WEBB: My name is Alanna Robertson-Webb, a horror-specializing author who is terrified of sharks and finds fun in editing character backstories for her Dungeons and Dragons group. I live with a fiancee and two cats, all of whom like to take over my favorite cozy blanket when they think they can get away with it. I am currently a wound vac specialist by day, and an editor and author by candlelight. One of the anthologies I am featured in, Monsters by Black Hare Press, was nominated for a 2019 Bram Stoker award. You can check out my work here, much of which has hit #1 spots on Amazon in various categories throughout 2019. https://arwauthor.wixsite.com/arwauth https://www.amazon.com/Alanna-Robertson-Webb/e/ B07LFYJYS5%3Fref=dbs_a_mng_rwt_scns_share

ALICE DE SAMPAIO is a Gothic Horror and Dark Fantasy author. When she's not writing her next novel she is probably at university or at home reading anything from Romanticism to Dystopian Comics. She is based in Antwerp, Belgium. ravensandbooks.tumblr.com https://alicedesampaio.blogspot.com/p/readers-list.html

AMBER M. SIMPSON is a dark speculative fiction writer with a penchant for horror and fantasy. She has been published in various anthologies, as well as online and in magazines. She assists in editing for Fantasia Divinity Magazine where she has gotten to work with many talented authors from all over the world. Though she loves to create dark worlds and diverse characters, her greatest creations of all are her two sons, who keep her feet on the ground, even while her head is in the clouds. Find her

online at her website: https://ambermsimpson.com/
https://www.facebook.com/authorambermsimpson/

ANDRA DILL: When not daydreaming about plot lines and characters Andra writes in multiple genres—including but not limited to—urban fantasy, steamy romance, paranormal romance, and horror.
www.facebook.com/andradillauthor and Twitter @aedill

ANDREW ANDERSON is a full-time civil servant from Bathgate, Scotland, writing fiction in his limited spare time. His work can be found online at FlashFlood and Re:Written, and published in Black Hare Press, Blood Song Books and Sampson Low anthologies. Twitter: @soorploom

ANDY LEAVY is a storyteller from Ardee, Ireland. He primarily writes Graphic Novels and Short Stories but plans to venture out into other mediums in time he has been reading and writing ever since his mother introduced him to books at a young age. When he is not reading or writing he can be found playing video games or honing his jiu-jitsu on the mats of 10th Planet Dublin. He can be found on Twitter: @midniteauth0r and on Facebook:
https://www.facebook.com/LeavyWriting/

ANN WYCOFF lives among the redwoods near Santa Cruz, California. She pines for the steaming jungles within the island kingdom of the imagination, where beats the heart of savage drums, and there live philosophic yet murderous crustaceans, shattered robots, buried sacrifices to forgotten devils, and dark countries yet unfounded. Her short fiction and poetry have or will soon appear in Organic Ink Volume 2, Scary Snippets Christmas Edition, and the Porter Gulch Review. She can be reached through her blog, Ann's Immaterium, at www.annwycoff.com.

ARNIE MAY is a writer from North Carolina. He grew up on a steady diet of horror and humor; this explains his love for clowns. Currently, he's all about rainy days, cigars, and good stories. You can find him on Twitter: @arnie_may

BRIAN ROSENBERGER lives in a cellar in Marietta, GA and writes by the light of captured fireflies. He is the author of As the Worm Turns and three poetry collections - Poems That Go Splat, And For My Next Trick..., and Scream for Me. He is also a featured contributor to the must-read Pro-Wrestling literary collection, Three-Way Dance, available from Gimmick Press.
https://www.facebook.com/HeWhoSuffers
 https://www.instagram.com/brianrosenberger7097

BRYAN DYKE lives and works in Northern Vermont with his wife and two children. A graduate of the University of Florida, he has had several stories published in small press anthologies over the last three years, most recently a tale in DMR's Anthology " Death Dealers and Diabolists" in the summer of 2019. He loves "Sword and Sorcery" and is heavily influenced by the likes of Jack Kirby, Robert Howard and Lovecraft.

C. MARRY HULTMAN is a teacher, writer and sometimes podcaster who is equal parts Swede and Wisconsinite. He

lives with his wife and two daughters and runs W.A.R.G –
The Guild podcast and his own creative website
Wisconsin Noir – Cosmic Horror set in the Dairy State.
Find out more about him at
https://wisconsinnoir.wixsite.com/wi

CALLUM PEARCE is a Dutch storyteller, originally from
Liverpool. Lover of the magical as well as the macabre
and about to appear in a few anthologies and drabble
collections. He lives in a foggy old fishing town in the
Netherlands with his husband and a couple of cat shaped
sprites. Twitter: https://mobile.twitter.com/Aladdinsane79
Facebook: https://m.facebook.com/calmpeace13/

CHARLES REIS was born and raised in Coventry, Rhode
Island, but currently lives in West Warwick. He graduated
from the University of Rhode Island with a BA in English
Literature in 2012, although he currently works as a
museum tour guide. Additional works of his have
appeared in "One Night in Salem", "Trembling with Fear:
Year 1" and "Coffins & Dragons".
Facebook: https://www.facebook.com/charles.reis.35
Instagram: https://www.instagram.com/cthulhudawn1979/

CHARLOTTE O'FARRELL is a horror writer. A lifelong fan
of the genre, she wants to share her love for all things
weird and wonderful with her readers. She lives in
Nottingham, UK with her husband, daughter and cat. She
writes daily flash fiction on Twitter (@ChaOFarrell) and
Facebook (@AuthorCharlotteOFarrell).

CHRIS BANNOR is a science fiction, fantasy, and horror writer who lives in Southern California. Chris learned her love of genre stories from her mother at an early age and has never veered far from that path. She also enjoys musical theater and road trips with her family but is a general homebody otherwise. You can follow Chris on Facebook @chrisbannorauthor or www.ChrisBannor.com

CHRIS HEWITT resides in the beautiful garden of England, Kent UK and in the odd moments that he isn't dog walking, he pursues his passion for all things horror, fantasy and science-fiction. Twitter: @i_mused_blog Blog: http://mused.blog/

CLINT FOSTER lives with his herd of four cats, beloved Basset Hound, Zero, and wonderful wife, Nik, in southern Iowa. He loves telling stories as much as he does reading them, and is excited to share his tales with the world. www.facebook.com/clintfosterauthor

DAVID A.F. BROWN is a Canadian author whose fiction has appeared in various anthologies, magazines and podcasts, including Tales to Terrify, Deep Fried Horror, Forest of Fear – Volume 1 and Love: Dark Drabbles #7. He was a finalist in the NYC Midnight Short Story Challenge 2019, an international competition of over 4,500 writers. He holds a BA (Hons) from Western University and resides in Caledon, Ontario, with his wife and son. You can find David A.F. Brown on Facebook at: www.facebook.com/browndavidaf

DEREK DUNN is a film enthusiast and musician who writes primarily horror and mystery stories. After obtaining a degree in Media Arts Studies and dabbling in film production, he's turned his efforts to writing fiction. Several of his works have appeared in recent anthologies. He lives in the American northwest with his family, dog, and fish. Twitter: @DerekTDunn

DICKON SPRINGATE hails from the town of Gillingham in Kent, UK, where he lives with his Mexican wife and enjoys watching movies and trying as many new board games as he can find. He has had numerous forays into the world of the written word, most recently founding the indie publishing house Beyond Death Publishing, which published its first anthology in April 2019 and currently has almost a dozen more ideas on the script-board, ensuring that he will be very busy for the foreseeable future.

DREW STARLING is an author of horror and dark fiction. His short stories have been featured in nearly a dozen published anthologies and his collaborative novel "Storming Area 51: Horror at the Gate" spent time ranked as Amazon's #1 Sci-Fi Anthology. You can find him on Twitter @ScaryStarling. His only rule of writing is the dog never dies.

ELIN OLAUSSON is a bookaholic and a librarian, which means she's reading constantly (or wishing she was). Somehow she finds the time to write too. Her favorite genre is horror, which is ironic since she's scared of everything. Her stories frequently feature dysfunctional

families, disturbed minds, and woods as dark as the ones surrounding the village where she grew up. She lives in Sweden. Elin also writes LGBT romance under the pen name Elvira Bell. Website: www.elinolausson.com
 Twitter: @elin_writes

ELIZABETH NETTLETON studied Law at the Queensland University of Technology, Australia, and now lives with her family in Oxford, UK. She enjoys writing dark fiction, horror and fantasy stories, and her work has most recently appeared in The Sirens Call eZine.
Twitter - @ElizabethNett18
https://elizabeth-nettleton.webnode.com/

EMMA K. LEADLEY is a UK-based writer, creative geek, and devourer of words, images and ideas. She began writing both fiction and creative non-fiction as an outlet for her busy brain, and quickly realised scrawling words on a page is wired into her DNA. Visit her online at www.emmaleadley.co.uk
www.twitter.com/autoerraticism

FAITH PIERCE is from Texas originally and now lives in the Midwest. She works in marketing and writes web content by day. The rest of the time, she writes horror, speculative fiction, and whatever else pops into her head or gives her nightmares. Find her on Twitter @faithepierce.

FRED WILLIAMSON is a writer and poet from Massachusetts with a vested interest in the macabre and the strange. When he is not attending local metal shows, he can be found building new worlds and characters to torment in them. He is survived by his cat.

GABRIELLA BALCOM lives in Texas with her family, loves reading and writing, and thinks she was born with a book in her hands. She works in a mental health field, and writes fantasy, horror/thriller, romance, children's stories, sci-fi, and more. She likes traveling, music, good shows, photography, history, genealogy, interesting tales, and animals. Gabriella says she's a sucker for a great story and loves forests, mountains, and back roads which might lead who knows where. She has a weakness for lasagna, garlic bread, tacos, cheese, and chocolate, but not necessarily in that order, and she loves Mexican, Chinese, and Italian food. You can check out her author page at: https://m.facebook.com/GabriellaBalcom.lonestarauthor

GRANT HINTON is the wifi password to the world of horror. His technological knowledge mixed with the grasp of the human condition results in devastatingly chilling results. Not only that, this bestselling author is hauntingly gifted in all things to raise the hairs on the back of your neck, all the ways to quickening your heartbeat, and leave you with a lesson that stays long after your eyes have left his words. There are great things on the horizon coming ahead, stay tuned for more soul gripping content. https://www.facebook.com/granthintonauthor https://www.twitter.com/granthinton3

GALINA TREFIL is a novelist specializing in women's, minority, and disabled rights. Her short stories and articles have appeared in Neurology Now, UnBound

Emagazine, The Guardian, Tikkun, Romea.CZ, Jewcy, Jewrotica, Telegram Magazine, Ink Drift Magazine, The Dissident Voice, Open Road Review, and the anthologies "Flock: The Journey," "First Love," "Sea of Secrets," "Coffins and Dragons," "Organic Ink volume One," "Winds of Despair," "Waters of Destruction," "Curses & Cauldrons," and "Suspense Unimagined."
https://www.facebook.com/Rabbi-Galina-Trefil-535886443115467/
https://galinatrefil.wordpress.com/

HANNAH HULBERT lives in urban Dorset, UK. She is on a permanent sabbatical from reality as she raises two children and devotes her time to visiting imaginary worlds, some of her own creation. You can find her short stories in the British Fantasy Society's Horizons,the anthologies Curse of the Gods (ed. Sarah Gribble), Once and Future Moon (ed. Allen Ashley) and the forthcoming Beneath Strange Stars (TL;DR Press). She is probably tweeting or doodling at this very moment on Twitter here: @hhulbert

HEIDI ANN WILLITS is an aspiring YA Fantasy novelist who enjoys spending her free time making stuff up. She is currently a senior in the Bachelor's of Art Creative Writing program at Southern New Hampshire University and specializes in fiction. She enjoys spending her time creatively, working in the marketing field and collaborating with brand owners. Find her on Twitter @heidiwillits or on Facebook by searching Heidi Ann Willits to keep up with her updates on her writing progress and upcoming projects.

HEINRICH VON WOLFCASTLE writes by candlelight from the seclusion of his castle in the foothills of the Carpathian Mountains. An unofficial paranormal investigator and horror writer, his debut anthology of short stories titled Screams Before Dawn was released in September of 2018 and was called "an engaging page turner," by Scream Magazine. He is an affiliate member of the Horror Writers Association and a member of the Great Lakes Association of Horror Writers. Though he lives the life of a recluse, he has been known to emerge from the shadows for Trick-or-Treaters on Halloween night. And he updates his blog regularly here:

https://www.heinrichvonwolfcastle.com/blog

HENRY HERZ wrote the children's books: MONSTER GOOSE NURSERY RHYMES (Pelican), WHEN YOU GIVE AN IMP A PENNY (Pelican), MABEL & THE QUEEN OF DREAMS (Schiffer), LITTLE RED CUTTLEFISH (Pelican), CAP'N REX & HIS CLEVER CREW (Sterling), HOW THE SQUID GOT TWO LONG ARMS (Pelican), ALICE'S MAGIC GARDEN (Familius), GOOD EGG AND BAD APPLE (Schiffer), 2 PIRATES + 1 ROBOT (Kane Miller), THE MAGIC SPATULA (Month9 Books), and I AM SMOKE (Tilbury House). He authored the stories: "Gluttony" in CLASSICS REMIXED anthology (Left Hand Publishing), "Zombie Sonnet 43", "Forbidden Love", and "Blind Date" in MONSTERS anthology (Black Hare Press), "All the World's a Shipwreck" and "Lend Me Your Arms" in 100 WORD ZOMBIE BITES anthology (Reanimated Writers Press), and "Pay the Piper" (Highlights for Children).
Website: https://www.henryherz.com

Facebook: https://www.facebook.com/henry.herz/

HOLLEY CORNETTO was born and raised in Alabama, but now lives in New Jersey. To indulge her love of books and stories, she became a librarian. She is also a writer, because the only thing better than being surrounded by stories is to create them herself. She can be found lurking on Twitter @HLCornetto.

HUNTER LACROSS: Greetings lords and ladies I am Hunter of the LaCross clan. My passions include larping, football, and spending time with close friends. When I'm not doing those three things there is a good chance I am either watching a movie, relaxing with my fiancé Alanna, or cooking us a fantastic dinner. U/XxAtroticusxX

JACEK WILKOS is an engineer from Poland. He lives with his wife and daughter in a beautiful city of Cracow. He is addicted to buying books, he loves coffee, dark ambient music and riding his bike. He writes mostly horror drabbles. His fiction in Polish can be read on Szortal, Niedobre literki, Horror Online. In English his work was published in Drablr, Rune Bear, Sirens Call eZine, Trembling With Fear, and in numerous anthologies, both in print and ebook. My facebook author page: https://www.facebook.com/Jacek.W.Wilkos/

JACLYN FULSCHER is a first-year studying English-Creative Writing at Butler University. Jaclyn grew up on crime based TV shows and children's horror novels. She has always had a passion for creative writing and continues to love dark literature to this day.

JEN CHICHESTER is a misfit toy who enjoys learning, reading, and writing about anything oddball, eccentric, eclectic, mysterious, mystical, mythical, magical, and macabre. She is a native of West Michigan but feels more at home in the United Kingdom. She has her Master's in English from Grand Valley State University and has a special interest in literary perspectives on madness. While not working as a freelancer, she writes, reads, fangirls over Twin Peaks, and chases around after kids and critters. https://www.facebook.com/JenChichesterWritesStuff/ Instagram: @hopelesspierrot

JENNIFER WINTERS is a writer of dark fiction, horror, and low fantasy, with elements of magical realism and the weird. Originally from Alcorn County, Mississippi, she currently resides in Central Maryland. Her work has been featured in various publications, and on the NoSleep Podcast and The Grey Rooms Podcast. She can be found on Twitter @wordywinters.

JESS RHODES is a biologist and a speculative fiction/horror writer. Sometimes those things get a little too entwined…. She lives in Northern California with her partner and their menagerie. You can find her on Twitter @dead_end_rhodes.

JIM BATES: Jim lives in a small town twenty miles west of Minneapolis, Minnesota. His stories have appeared online in CafeLit, The Writers'; Cafe Magazine, Cabinet of Heed, Paragraph Planet, Nailpolish Stories, Ariel Chart, Potato Soup Journal, Literary Yard, Spillwords (Dec, 2019, Author of the Month), The Drabble and World of

Myth Magazine. In print publications: A Million Ways, Mused Literary Journal, Gleam Flash Fiction Anthology #2 by Clarendon House Publishing, The Best of CafeLit 8 and the Nativity Anthology by Bridge House Publishing and Gold Dust Magazine. You can also check out his blog to see more: www.theviewfromlonglake.wordpress.com

JOE SCIPIONE: A high school teacher for twelve years, Joe currently lives in Illinois with his wife and two kids. He has had several short stories published in various anthologies and magazines. He is a book reviewer and Senior Contributor at HorrorBound.net. You can follow him on twitter @JoeScipione0 or on Instagram: JoeScipione0

JOEL R HUNT is a writer from the British Midlands who has a passion for horror, science fiction and all things bizarre. Joel's drabbles and other short stories can be found in a range of anthologies by Black Hare Press, Fantasia Divinity and Escaped Ink, among others.
He also posts daily micro stories on
https://twitter.com/JoelRHunt1
and a number of longer stories and poems on
https://www.reddit.com/r/JRHEvilInc/.

JOSH HERZ co-authored the children's books: MONSTER GOOSE NURSERY RHYMES, WHEN YOU GIVE AN IMP A PENNY, MABEL & THE QUEEN OF DREAMS, and LITTLE RED CUTTLEFISH. His horror short stories "Band of Brothers" and "The Road Not Taken" appear in the APOCALYPSE anthology from Black Hare Press. His dioramas, Zombie Apocalypse, The Doorways of Life, and Band of Brothers, appeared in Cicada Magazine.

JOSHUA E. BORGMANN holds degrees from Drake University, Iowa State University, and the University of South Carolina. He grew up on horror and science-fiction and had long intended to become a great master of the art form before he was sucked into the bottomless pit of academia. He toils away his days as an English instructor at a small community college and dreams of being able to escape into a world of fantasy and terror where there are no student papers to grade. He and his wife reside in a nameless rural Iowa town surrounded by terrible cornfields where he is terrorized by several felines who have taken refuge in his home.

K.B. ELIJAH is a fantasy author living in Brisbane, Australia, with her husband and three cockatiels. A lawyer by day, and a writer by...also day, because she needs her solid nine hours of sleep per night (not that the cockatiels let her sleep past 6am). She believes that if writing and reading aren't fun and full of surprises, then something has gone wrong. Her anthology of short fantasy stories with twists, The Empty Sky, is available on paperback and Kindle now. Find her on Twitter at @KBElijah1 or Instagram at @k.b.elijah for book reviews, promotions and cute bird photos.

K. R. NOX is an Australian short story writer of the Horror and Thriller genres with a Paranormal twist. A love of ancient myths, legends and the occult means there is always something dark brewing on the horizon.
Website: www.krnox.com

K.T. Tate lives in Cambridgeshire in the UK. She writes mainly weird fiction, cosmic horror and strange monster stories. More info and publication history can be found at https://eldritch-hollow.com/

Karen Heslop writes from Kingston, Jamaica. Her stories can be found in Apparition Lit Mag, The Weird and Whatnot and Haunted MTL among others. She tweets @kheslopwrites. Twitter handle: @kheslopwrites

Kase Glidewell is a history major at the University of Central Missouri. He is an aspiring (and now published) writer of science fiction, fantasy, and horror. He began writing in elementary and has been at it ever since. When Kase isn't studying or writing, he likes to rock climb, watch soccer, and read.

You can follow him at https://twitter.com/kaseman742 on twitter and https://www.instagram.com/kaseman742/ on Instagram.

Kathleen Halecki possesses a B.A. and M.A. in history, and a doctoral degree in interdisciplinary studies. Although born in New York, she currently resides in a seventeenth century home in New England. Although preferring to remain elusive and private, she does have a Facebook account. Her stories are included in, Shadows in Salem: Wicked Tales from the Witch City; One Night in Salem; Midnight Rising: A Collection of Paranormal Tales; From a Cat's View Volume II, and Shadow of Pendle. She has also drabbled in Curses and Cauldrons, Forest of Fear, and the forthcoming, Hate and Nano Nightmares.

KERRY E.B. BLACK writes from the fog-enshrouded realm outside the city of steel and zombies in Pennsylvania. Her writing often explores the connection between fear and the monsters that inevitably act as cautionary elements. Her debut novel, "Season of Secrets," is available through B&N, Amazon, at https://kerrylizblack.wordpress.com/, and Audible. Selected short stories compiled in "Herd of Nightmares" and "Carousel of Nightmares" are bound by and available through Tree Shadow Press and Amazon. https://www.goodreads.com/author/show/7874880.Kerry_E_B_Black https://twitter.com/BlackKerryblick

KEVIN J KENNEDY is a horror author & editor from Scotland. He is the co-author of You Only Get One Shot, Screechers and has a solo collection available called Dark Thoughts. He is also the publisher of several bestselling anthology series; Collected Horror Shorts, 100 Word Horrors & The Horror Collection, as well as the stand-alone anthology Carnival of Horror. His stories have been featured in many other notable books in the horror genre. He lives in a small town in Scotland, with his wife and his two little cats, Carlito and Ariel. Keep up to date with new releases or contact Kevin through his website: www.kevinjkennedy.co.uk

KIM PLASKET is a Jersey girl at heart relocated to sunny Florida. She enjoys writing mainly horror and paranormal stories and lives with her husband and 2 kids. When she is not slaving away at her day job, she can be found drinking coffee with fellow author Valerie Willis and planning the demise of some poor character. Currently, she has several short stories featured in anthologies such as 'Demonic Wildlife' and 'The Hunted', also has a story in an Anthology Titled Fireflies and Fairy dust she also has had a story featured in Shades of Santa. Also the newly released DrabbleDark Anthology, Work of hearts magazine. She has stories in Trembling With Fear, more tales from the tree. Just released. The thrill of the Hunt: Buried Alive. Coming out later this year Demonic Carnival: First Ticket's free. She also has several short stories and a post for Women in Horror Month on the website The Horror Tree.

https://www.amazon.com/-/e/B074YCLRCF

KIMBERLY REI has been writing for as long as she can remember. At five years old, her parents gifted her with a set of Children's Classics that she had no hope of reading. Yet. The potential alone sparked a love of words that has never wavered. Kim has taught writing workshops and edited novels for Authors You May Recognize. She has published several short stories and now can't stop chasing paper dragons. She currently lives in Tampa Bay, Florida with her wife and an abundance of gorgeous beaches to explore. http://tales.studiorei.org/

LAURENCE SULLIVAN: Runner-up in the Wicked Young Writer Awards: Gregory Maguire Award, Laurence Sullivan's creative writing has appeared in such places as: Londonist, The List, NHK-World, Literary Orphans and Crack the Spine. He became inspired to start writing during his studies at the universities of Kent, Utrecht and Birmingham – after being saturated in all forms of literature from across the globe and enjoying every moment of it. He is currently pursuing a PhD at

Northumbria University in the Medical Humanities, exploring literary portrayals of women's domestic medicine during the eighteenth century. More of his work can be found online at www.laurencesullivan.co.uk and on Twitter @LozzySullivan

LP HERNANDEZ is an author of horror and speculative fiction. His stories are featured in many collections, including Tavistock Galleria, Black Rainbow, and Monstronomicon. His work has also been adapted as audio productions on the NoSleep Podcast. He is an NYC Midnight Short Story Challenge Finalist and was awarded second place in the 2019 Writer's Digest Annual Writing Competition. www.lphernandez.com

MARK ANTHONY SMITH was born in Hull, East Yorkshire. His poems and short stories have appeared in Spelk, Truly U and Nymphs with more to follow in The Cabinet of Heed and Pink Plastic House. Hearts of the matter is available on Amazon.
Facebook: Mark Anthony Smith-Author
Twitter: MarkAnthonySm16

MARK KODAMA is a trial attorney and former newspaper reporter who lives in Washington, D.C. with his wife and two sons. He is currently working on Las Vegas Tales, a work of philosophy, sugar-coated with meter and rhyme and told through stories. His 100 short stories, poems and essays have been published in anthologies, including those published by Clarendon Publishing House, Black Hare Press and Devil's Party Press, and literary magazines and journals.

MATT LUCAS: I am an author represented by Labyrinth Literary Agency. I delve into paranormal, fantasy, sci-fi, and horror. My debut novel, The Shadow Gospels, is currently being pitched to publishers. I've had several short stories published with Black Hare Press, Blood Song Books, and Eerie River Publishing. As my career progresses, I'm always looking for opportunities to expand my resume. Writing is my passion and I hope to spend my days cultivating captivating stories with impactful messages. https://twitter.com/MattDLuke https://www.instagram.com/mattdluke/?hl=en

MATTHEW A. CLARKE is a new face in the world of horror. He has been writing short fiction as a hobby for two years and has decided to share his passion with likeminded people. Matthew loves all things that go bump in the night, having been introduced to slasher movies at a young age. He lives on the South Coast of England with his fiancé, Isabelle, and a little dachshund called Frank. Matthew's story, Worth It, is soon to be published in 100 Word Horrors 4. You can find more about Matthew and updates on his upcoming works at www.facebook.com/fotc87

MELODY GRACE is a writer of all things terrifying and unsettling. She began her journey to the dark side at a very young age, as a way to bring her fears to life. As you read her stories, you will find that her dreams are now your nightmares, as she sweeps you into the dark realm of horror. You can frequently find her work on Reddit's horror platform: NoSleep, along with many different podcasts. This year alone she has been published in many terrifying anthologies, as well as her very own: Nocturnal Nightmares. Https://www.facebook.com/nocturnalnanny/ Https://www.twitter.com/nocturnalnanny/

MICHAEL D. NADEAU: Born in the usual way, author Michael D. Nadeau found fantasy at the age of 8 with Dungeons & Dragons. He loved being different people as well as casting magic and in time he discovered his love for reading. He has read hundreds of fantasy books, living in each of their worlds, and after awhile, he created his own. He is the author of the Lythinall series: The Darkness Returns book 1, The Darkness Within book 2 (June 2020) & The Darkness Falls (coming soon), and has several stories in Kyanite Press's Journal of speculative fiction. His stories all connect and intertwine, but be careful, they don't always let you leave after you read them. https://karsisthebard.wordpress.com/

MICHELLE RIVER: Michelle has always had a creative spirit and has a passion for painting, photography, pottery and writing. To her husband's dismay, she is happiest when she has three projects on the go, revelling in the chaos around her. Michelle hails from Ontario, Canada where she is lives with her wonderful husband and fearless daughter. A lover of hot black coffee and everything dark and terrifying, she spends her nights writing horror and dreaming about all things that go bump in the night.
www.Facebook.com/MichelleRiverAuthor/

N.M. BROWN is an international best selling author from Florida. She's a happily married mother who sheds light on the dark corners of the mind that we like to keep hidden. Her other publications include stories in each of Sirens at Midnight, Calls From the Brighter Futures Suicide Hotline, Fantasia Divinity's Elemental Drabble Series, the Scary Snippets Collections, the Mother Ghost Grimm children's horror anthology, Dark Xmas, along with several others being released in the next year.

NERISHA KEMRAJ: Short-fiction Author, and Poet, Nerisha Kemraj - resides in Durban, South Africa with her husband and two mischievous daughters. When she isn't writing, she is the master of procrastination. She has work published/accepted in various publications - both print and online. She holds a Bachelor's degree in Communication Science, and a Post Graduate Certificate in Education from the University of South Africa. Some of her published work can be found here:
https://www.amazon.com/author/nerisha_kemraj
https://www.facebook.com/pg/Nerishakemrajwriter/
https://www.instagram.com/nerishakemraj

NICK MOORE is a lawyer, veteran, and a lifelong lover of horror. He believes firmly that spiders are horrifying and the dog should always survive the story. Nick originally hails from New England and now lives in the Blue Ridge Mountains with his wife and rescue animals. His work can be found at www.nmwrites.com.

NOA COVO is an aspiring teenage writer. Her work has been published in "Museum Anthology", a Didcot Writers anthology, and in the fourth issue of "Reckoning". She can be found on Twitter @covo_noa.

PADDY ARMSTRONG is a student in central Maryland. In addition to writing, he is also a musician and an athlete. Paddy is a lover of H.P. Lovecraft and mythology, mostly that of Norse and Japanese culture.

PATRICIA ELLIOTT lives in Beautiful British Columbia with her family. Now that her lovely kids are all teenagers, she has decided to actively pursue her passion for the written word. When she was a youngster, she spent the majority of her time writing fan-fiction and poetry to avoid the harsh reality of bullying. Writing allowed her to escape into another world, even if temporarily; a world in which she could be anyone or anything, even a mermaid. Dreams really can come true. If you believe it, you can achieve it!
https://www.facebook.com/AuthorPatriciaElliott
https://www.twitter.com/AuthorPatricia

PAUL BENKENDORFER is an English and history teacher from Scottsdale Arizona. Paul has been working with at-risk youth and special needs children for over 13 years. Paul has been published in several journals including Allegory Ridge, The Write Launch, The Jewish Times, The Sports Haven, the Tucson Citizen, and the Silicon Journal. Paul received his B.A. in Creative Writing from the University of Arizona and is currently obtaining has Master's at Johns Hopkins University.
https://twitter.com/PBenkendorfer

REGINA KENNEY: Originally from Minnesota, Regina Kenney is a former reporter for Aviation Week magazine. Kenney moved to London in 2016 where she continued to

write for several blog sites including the Literature site, Literati Pulp, and the travel website, Love Pop Ups London. Kenney now lives in Dublin, Ireland where she continues to write short horror stories and poems. Her most recently published work is the short story, "Little Bone Brittle," which appeared in the 2019 horror anthology, Hamthology.
Twitter @Regina_Kenney
Instagram @Regina_Kenney

ROBIN BRAID writes stories of the mysterious and macabre. A resident of Fife, Scotland, he graduated from Dundee University with a degree in English Literature. When not working in his regular job, he can often be found rambling over hills and glens in search of inspiration for further weird tales.
www.twitter.com/robinbraid

RON DAVIS: Although relatively new to writing Ron has been a lifelong reader, specifically of the horror and dark fiction genres. He is a proud supporter of indie horror authors and artists. Ron lives in the dark woods of Pennsylvania with his wife and three sons. Ron can be contacted via Facebook at
https://www.facebook.com/RonDavisAuthor
or Twitter @RonDavis1980.

RUSSELL SMEATON: Born from an egg on a mountain top, Russell has spent the past 40 something years doing stuff and things. After spending a decade travelling around the world he has now settled down in the North of England. He lives with his lovely family and a few errant cats, who know far more than they should. Luckily they're not telling.

https://www.amazon.co.uk/Russell-Smeaton/e/B06XSYJ8TP

https://www.facebook.com/tikirussy/

RYAN ROSENBERRY is a short story writer who braves the tundra known as Fargo, North Dakota, along with his wife, son, two cats and a spoiled, Japanese chin. When not writing, you may find Ryan running the trails, exploring the outdoors, or sneaking off to Las Vegas. He is previous publish on the artist to authors project on the Immortal Artist Website.

S. C. MORGAN lives in Ontario, Canada with his family spending his days working for a bank and most nights putting pen to paper. His stories have appeared in the Unleashed: Monsters Vs Zombies anthology and the Forgotten Ones: Drabbles of Myth and Legend. For more information about his stories, you can follow him on Twitter at @SCMorganAuthor and on Facebook at www.facebook.com/SCMorganAuthor/

SANDY BUTCHERS is an author and an artist, known for her elaborate fantasy worlds and creature-designs. After living in Scandinavia for a year, she is now settled in the countryside, with a variety of pets and maps on which X marks the spot. She started her writing career at a very young age. After her first publication at the age of 14, writing has been a part of her life ever since. Anything from short stories and articles, to full-length novels have rolled off her keyboard. Today she teaches technology, and

runs an art center for teenagers and youngsters. When she doesn't stand in front of a classroom, she sits behind a computer, typing away on fantastical worlds filled with shape-shifters, witches and fairytales. For more info, please visit http://www.sandybutchers.com
https://www.facebook.com/AuthorSandyButchers/

SARAH MATTHEWS is a writer of fantasy/horror/humor from New Albany, Indiana. By day, she's a social worker. By night, she's writing or watching ASMR videos, or both at the same time. Find her on Twitter @superbfinch.

SEAN P. CHATTERTON writes fiction with a hope that you will remember the story long after you have finished reading it. Like the world famous grandfather of modern SF, Arthur C. Clarke, his first published short story was of a teleporter accident. This was sheer coincidence but one that Sean is very proud of. He now produces short stories on a regular basis and has had over twenty published stories to his credit.
http://www.seanpchatterton.co.uk
https://www.facebook.com/sean.p.chatterton

SHELDON WOODBURY is an award winning writer (screenplays, plays, books, short stories, and poems). His book "Cool Million" is considered the essential guide to writing high concept movies. His short stories and poems have appeared in many horror anthologies and magazines. His novel "The World on Fire" was published September, 2014 by JWK Fiction. His poem, The Midnight Circus, was selected by Ellen Datlow as an honorable mention for Best Horror 2017.

Amazon page:

https://www.amazon.com/Sheldon-Woodbury/e/B001K86VBI?ref=sr_ntt_srch_lnk_1&qid=1575672148&sr=1-1

Blog: http://sheldonwoodbury.blogspot.com/

STACEY JAINE MCINTOSH lives in Perth, Western Australia with her husband and four children. Although her first love has always been writing, she once toyed with being a Cartographer and subsequently holds a Diploma in Spatial Information Services. Since 2011, she has had over thirty short stories and twenty-two poems published. Stacey is also the author of Solstice Morrighan, Lost & Le Fay. When not with her family or writing she enjoys reading, genealogy, history, Arthurian myths and witchcraft. Visit her at: www.staceyjainemcintosh.com

STEVE STRED writes dark, bleak horror fiction. He is the author of the novels Invisible, The Stranger and Piece of Me. He has released six novellas including The One That Knows No Fear from Demain Publishing. He has also released four collections of stories, poems and drabbles. He has had works featured in Aphotic Realm, 100 Word Horrors 3, 100 Word Zombie Bites and Forest of Fear Vol 1.Steve lives in Edmonton, AB, Canada with his wife, son and dog OJ.

www.stevestredauthor.wordpress.com

www.amazon.com/author/stevestred

T.J. LEA is a British horror writer best known for penning the Creepypasta sensation "The Expressionless" back in 2012. A well known name in the online horror space, he has since then released several viral short stories through the NoSleep platform and gained a cult following. He is also heavily involved in the British Wrestling scene as a commentator and manager, he can be found on his facebook page /tjayleawriter or on twitter @tjaylea. TJ is releasing his debut novel "The Spaces In Between" based on his viral NoSleep Series through Eerie River Publishing this August

THOMAS WAKE was born into the harsh winters in the Nordic Finland. Tempered by the shamanic winds, thousand lakes with a thousand stories, the whispers of the birch filled forests, he fell in love with horror at the render age of 6 when he saw Re-Animator. That led him to search for the source story and that was it. Cosmic horror wrapped it's nebulous tentacles around his imagination and it has been feeding it ever since. Consuming book after book, he realized his dream; to be a writer. And that dream has guided him his entire life. Twitter: https://twitter.com/ThomasWake12

TIMOTHY FRIESENHAHN: My debut horror novel, Cold Fear released earlier this month under Terrotract Publishing LLC. I am a non-radical vegan who works construction and writes horror stories. I live in central Texas with my fiance and two little misbehaved dogs. twitter/@timfriesenhahn https://www.facebook.com/timot hy.friesenhahn.7

TOR-ANDERS ULVEN is a father, husband, and horror fiction writer hailing from the cold mountains of Norway. He became known through his horror alter ego

hyperobscure, primarily posting short stories on the vast writing subreddit of NoSleep. He has since had work published in several anthologies, and will continue to expand his dark universe for as long as people dare visit it.
Facebook: https://www.facebook.com/hyperobscure/
Reddit: https://www.reddit.com/user/hyperobscura

WENDY CHEAIRS lives in New Mexico, with her husband and cats that think they are little people. She works as an editor and freelance writer for longer than she'd care to admit. Now free to explore the fiction side of writing, diving into several different genres. Raised in the southwestern part of America, she hides from the desert sun in the writing cave to avoid setting ablaze. She is starting her publishing career with anthology work and working on novels.
https://www.facebook.com/AuthorWendyCheairs/
Website: https://indigowriter.com/

WILLEM V MUCH was born in Moscow in 1990, just as the Soviet Union collapsed. He had nothing to do with that. After reading too many books, he was sent to Denver, Colorado, where he devoured a library before moving on to the Internet. He still lives there. Willem's habitat:
https://twitter.com/VeryScholar

XIMENA ESCOBAR: Originally from Santiago, Ximena is the author of a translation into Spanish of the Broadway Musical ""The Wizard of Oz"" (2012) and of an original adaptation of the same, ""Navidad en Oz"" (2018), both produced in Chile. Since the latter she has dedicated herself to her writing, publishing poetry, short stories and drabbles, online and on print. Whilst poetry and literary are the genres which come most naturally, she is loving experimenting with horror, speculative fiction and fantasy, whilst working on a personal collection of stories.

She has a degree in Arts & Communication Science, and lives in Nottingham with her family. To follow her progress, you can find her on social media.

Facebook: @ximenautora.

YVONNE GLASGOW is a prolific published writer of short stories and poetry, from Grand Rapids, Michigan. Her first book was a children's picture book published in 2008. Yvonne works as a freelance writer and spends her spare time writing fiction and poetic spells, as well as crafting zodiac and divination art.

https://www.facebook.com/glassgoatpublishing/
https://www.facebook.com/dreamsanddivination/

ZOEY XOLTON is an Australian Speculative Fiction writer, primarily of Dark Fantasy, Paranormal Romance and Horror. She is also a proud mother of two, and is married to her soul mate. Outside of her family, writing is her greatest passion. She is especially fond of short fiction and is working on releasing her own themed collections in future. To find out more, please visit:

www.zoeyxolton.com!

DON'T MISS OUT!

Looking for additional content?
Becoming an exclusive Patreon member gives you
a chance to be a part of the action as well as giving you
creative content every single month, no matter the tier.
Vote on upcoming themes, extra author interview
questions, get free eBooks and in the higher tiers get
paperbacks sent to your home before they are even
released.

Here at Eerie River Publishing, we are focused on
providing paid writing opportunities for all indie authors.
Outside of our limited drabble collections we put out each
year, every single written piece that we publish -including
short stories featured in this collection have been paid for.

https://www.patreon.com/EerieRiverPub

Sign up for Eerie River Publishing's monthly newsletter to
get all the up to date information on new releases, author
interviews, book giveaways and so much more.
Sign up for our newsletter here.

https://mailchi.mp/71e45b6d5880/welcomebook

You can contact David Earth here:
earthtodavid101@gmail.com

If you leave a supporting review, it would be much appreciated.